Could I
Have My
Body Back
Now, Please?

COULD I
HAVE MY
BODY BACK
NOW, PLEASE?

BY BETH GOOBIE

NEWEST PRESS
EDMONTON

First edition

Canadian Cataloguing in Publication Data

Goobie, Beth, 1959 -
  Could I have my body back now, please?

  ISBN 0-920897-09-6

  I. Title.
  PS8563.062C6 1991   C813'.54   C91-091469-9
  PS9199.3.G66C6 1991

Credits
COVER & INTERIOR DESIGN: Bob Young/BOOKENDS DESIGNWORKS
EDITOR FOR THE PRESS: Douglas Barbour
FINANCIAL ASSISTANCE: NeWest Press gratefully acknowledges the
financial assistance of Alberta Culture and Multiculturalism, The
Alberta Foundation for the Literary Arts, The Canada Council, and
The NeWest Institute for Western Canadian Studies.

The author wishes to thank Sandra Birdsell for her editorial
assistance and Alberta Culture and Multiculturalism for a grant
which aided the writing of this book.

Printed and Bound in Canada by Gagné Printing Ltd., Toronto

NeWest Publishers Limited
#310-10359-82 Avenue
Edmonton, Alberta
T6E 1Z9

For Laura

previous publication credits:

the operation-*Secrets From The Orange Couch*
the very wrinkled lives of all the varied waterstons-
    The New Quarterly
the first gods-*Grain*
Answers-*Edmonton Journal* Literary Competition-first prize fiction
genetics-*Fiddlehead*
The Detachable Appendage-*The NeWest Review*, summer 1991
Answers-*Prairie Fire*, Fall 1991

CONTENTS

agnes's body is a barometer

agnes milwaukee felt the vietnam war
in her bones – mostly the right elbow.
she said it shot a sheer transparent pain
bright as grenade explosions
up her arm, whenever anyone got killed
over there. when the americans gave up
and came home, her arthritis
cleared up for a while. all in all,
she was glad when the cold war ended,
and she could stop wearing her parka.
then the whole watergate affair
put her under with migraines
she didn't see the likes of again
until the principal trust fund
thingamigummy.

when the battle at wounded knee
grew warts with black hairs on her forehead,
it made her realize how glad she was
she missed christopher's discovery
of north america. on further reflection
she added to this
the birth of calvin, the crusades,
and the invention of hockey.

agnes worries about the birthmark
that appeared on her left breast
with pinochet's coup. it spreads
like a bruise towards her throat

she stopped drinking coca cola,
said it gave her heartburn
and diarrhea
for days.

lately agnes has been in a wheelchair,
says she can't walk –
since reagan's first election
there's been a pain growing
in her ass.
this culminated during the gretzky trade
when she began defecating hockey pucks.
agnes was caught off guard
as generally she had not been
a sports fan.

agnes does not anticipate her future.
with the advent of free trade
some of her body parts
have begun to shift –
exchange positions.
first, it was a finger
for a toe,
next, head for pubic hair.
funny how the south of her body
seems to gain larger portions
for smaller sections sent to the north.
yesterday, it was a hangnail
for her nose, this morning
she found her clitoris
where her heart used to beat.

while she is now able to provide
almost any situation
with a delicate sexual innuendo,
through slight adjustment
of breast pocket pen or corsage,
she feels, nonetheless,
that living with one's heart
between one's legs
is a situation
for a much younger woman.

THE DETACHABLE APPENDAGE

One day, as Kurt was playing soccer with the guys from work, he felt something slither down one leg of his shorts. It was an odd sensation, and Kurt felt different, though he could not pinpoint how. Looking down, Kurt saw the wrinkled, flesh coloured appendage lying in the grass. This was a startling moment, and Kurt was not at all sure what to do. He had not heard of this sort of thing happening before, not even in leprosy cases or on science fiction radio programs.

He looked around. Fortunately, his team had just scored and were busy jumping, hugging and slapping hands. Quickly he reached down and scooped up the appendage. He had no pockets in his t-shirt or shorts, so he pulled open the elasticized waist of his shorts, and dropped the appendage in, hoping for the best. It meandered down to its original position and attached itself. Kurt decided things must be back to normal, and went on playing soccer.

Kurt did not go to see his doctor about the incident. He preferred to see it as an 'incident' rather than a 'tendency,' and at any rate, it had only happened once. He did not see the point in asking a doctor whether body parts commonly detached and reattached themselves at will. He had a feeling they did not. He had no interest in spending the rest of his life as the object of scientific experiments or articles in medical journals. He had never wanted to be in the *Guiness Book of World Records*.

Kurt figured the matter must be psychological. These sorts of things usually were. He wondered, briefly, if the applicable term was 'psychological' or 'psychotic,' but could not remember the difference. At any rate, he did not want to lie on a couch and talk to someone with a foreign accent and bifocals. Kurt was the kind of man who stood up to talk to waiters. He found that being physically lower than someone else made him sweat.

Kurt decided to forget the whole thing. And for a while, the appendage cooperated. Kurt stopped ducking into bathroom cubicles to check and confirm status. He relaxed.

Kurt worked as a stock boy at the Whyte Avenue Safeway store. His main interests in life were hockey, basketball, football, soccer, baseball, wrestling, archery, stock car racing, golf and fly fishing. He had recently married.

The next time the appendage detached itself, Kurt was in a mall, watching a pottery demonstration. Having just purchased an Oilers sweater, Kurt had been walking along, minding his own business. Then he saw the woman sitting at the potter's wheel, her hands at work with a lump of clay. She was forming a cylinder. Kurt found himself fascinated as the shape formed around space. He stared.

And then it fell off again. Feeling it wander down his inner thigh, Kurt's eyes bugged. Quickly, he crooked his ankle, so the appendage was caught between the inside of his pant leg and foot. Then he bent over and casually slipped it into the folds of the Oilers sweater.

Kurt beat a disconcerted retreat to the nearest men's washroom. He went into a cubicle and unzipped his pants. There was no indication as to the exact location for reattachment, no small red circle or an X to mark the spot. Kurt made a guess and pushed the correct end of the appendage against his body. Poking around with his fingers, he could not find a seam or a crack. Everything seemed to be normal.

Still, Kurt was worried. He was beginning to think this could be considered a 'tendency.' As he urinated, he came up with what he thought might be a viable solution. He would wear a jock strap at all times. He nodded, tucking the appendage away.

The next time the appendage went its own way, Mirabella, Kurt's wife, was out for the evening at her French literature class. Kurt, on his way to get another beer during a tv ad in the Oilers/Kings game, passed her studio. The door was open. He flicked on the light.

On the easel was a partially finished watercolor of an iris. Mirabella, working from the outside in, had left the centre of the iris incomplete, an unpainted space. Kurt found himself attracted to the unfinished nature of the iris's centre. He watched it, thinking it might shift, or move. At this point, the appendage, once again, detached itself.

Kurt was not wearing a jock strap, since it had been months since the last mishap. The appendage landed, in an ungraceful flop on the carpet, between his feet.

"Shit," he said.

He picked it up. He was about to attempt the reattachment process, when he noticed that his fingers left slight indentations in the surface of the appendage. He poked at it. Again, his fingers left an impression.

Kurt found that touching the appendage in its detached state produced sensations in his body – not sexual, exactly. Kurt did not recall feeling this way before. It was not painful but pleasurable, in a mind-bending sort of way . . . inside, somewhere. He poked at the appendage again. This was interesting. He felt as if something moved around . . . inside.

Kurt decided to experiment. He rolled the appendage between his palms, enjoying the sensation. He watched as the shape in his hands became thinner and longer, like plasticine. He rounded the tip so that it resembled one of Mirabella's brushes, in a fleshy sort of way.

Kurt carefully removed the iris from the easel so that he faced a fresh white surface. Mirabella had wrapped the paints in a plastic bag to keep them from drying out. Kurt unwrapped them, then dipped the tip of the appendage into a deep blue. He applied the blue to the paper.

As Kurt moved the blue paint across the paper in broad sweeps, he felt a correlating interior sensation – a soft, light stroke. He relaxed slightly and took a deep breath. It was as if a hand had moved around, gently sweeping things aside – things Kurt had not known were there. As a matter of fact, or fancy, Kurt had not ever thought much about inside stuff, and he did not really ponder it now. He just enjoyed the sensation of breathing deeply. He washed off the top of the appendage and dipped it into the yellow.

Kurt worked in a series of broad strokes, and when he was finished, he thought the picture might be construed as an abstract sunset. He felt very light, like a shell around broad, blending sweeps of color. The paint on the canvas began to run together.

He heard Mirabella come in. Quickly, he washed off the appendage, shook it so that it flopped back into its original shape, and dropped it into his pants. It reconnected in an appropriate manner.

Kurt realized he must have missed the end of the Oilers game. As Mirabella entered the studio, he felt suddenly shy, expecting ridicule. He crossed his arms over his chest and looked at the floor.

Mirabella set down her French books. She saw his dribbling abstract. He face lit up and she smiled.

"Kurt!" she said. "I love the colours. I like the motion – the sweep of the stroke."

Kurt felt the colours sigh and settle, expand slightly. That night, as he and Mirabella made love, the colours shifted, like the Northern Lights. He did not realize this sounded very much like adolescent poetry. He had never written poetry, even as an adolescent. He concentrated on one colour after another, finding Mirabella responded most to the deep indigo motion, its slow, broad curve.

The Safeway shelves were often depleted after long weekends. Kurt worked, shoving canned goods onto the shelves. Boxes of products stood in the aisle, waiting placement. Suddenly, he stopped. He looked at the empty spaces on the shelves, the way the cans of stewed tomatoes were stacked around them. There was something pleasing about the space, something that drew his eye.

Kurt studied the space, considering. It made the surrounding cans look almost pleasant. Why not, thought Kurt, leave a space between the stacks of canned tomatoes, in order to make the cans look more attractive? This would please the customer, who would buy more stewed tomatoes, and Safeway would make a greater profit.

Kurt's supervisor came by and yelled at Kurt for standing around doing nothing. He told Kurt to get back to filling the shelves. Kurt watched the supervisor leave with narrowed eyes. Supervisors were blockheads, he thought – just there to make sure all the spaces were shoved full of canned tomatoes . . . there to shove all the time in an employee's day full of work. Supervisors had lost their sense of a day's internal space.

Kurt was pleased with his concept. He shook his head, feeling sorry for the supervisor, his limitations, his so obviously unhappy life.

A month or so later, Kurt turned on the stereo and discovered Mirabella had left it on CBC FM. He was about to flip it to 630 CHED, when a chorale piece came on. There was something about it, some sort of inner space to the music that made Kurt leave it on, give it a try.

The announcer said something about Vaughan Williams. Kurt lay on his back and closed his eyes. There was a hollow shape to the music. As Kurt listened, he began to sense shapes between the notes, the movement of the notes around silence.

Once again, the appendage let go. Kurt stood up and shook his pant leg, watching as the appendage slid out onto the floor. He picked it up.

The music continued. Kurt grinned. He would have his way with this appendage.

Gently, he struck a finger down the middle, creating a tunnel through the centre of the appendage. The internal sensation was immediate – a great opening up, a sense of arctic space. Along the outside, he introduced a series of holes. It was as if a sequence of windows opened, connecting internal and external spaces. Kurt threw back his head and laughed.

He had moulded a flesh-coloured flute. Kurt was glad no one could see him – he probably looked like some kind of pervert. He placed the flesh-coloured mouthpiece section against his lips. Moving his fingers over the holes, he found he was able to produce different pitches. He turned off the stereo; it was difficult to play along with Vaughan Williams.

Thinking this probably qualified as a mystical experience, Kurt decided to approach it in a Buddhistic mode. He sat cross-legged on the floor, piping out odd disconnected intervals and rhythm. He was not sure whether the notes could be heard by the ear – if, for example, Mirabella could have heard them. Each note seemed to take place inside, centering and then spreading out slowly, not as sound, but as space. Each note expanded slowly, gently, formed its own lingering, shimmering sense of space. Then it faded, and the next note created a presence . . . or absence. Kurt could not determine which. He settled into a slow, dreamy blues melody and replayed this for hours.

Then Kurt realized he had to relieve himself. He went to the bathroom, attached the appendage and began to urinate. At this point, he saw he had forgotten to shake the appendage back into shape again. It was still full of holes. Urine began to splash all over the toilet, the walls, his pants.

"Shit," said Kurt.

He tried to pull the appendage off, but this hurt, and the appendage remained firmly attached. There was a smug look to it, and Kurt recalled, with a growing dismay, his naive decision to have his way with the appendage. This was probably the revenge of the appendage.

"Please," he hissed, pulling at it. It did not budge.

The appendage was losing the shape Kurt had given it, and the holes had become indistinguishable, but Kurt continued to worry. Mirabella must not know about this. She would think him some sort of freak. She would call the doctor, the psychiatrist, the *Guiness Book of World Records*. She would leave him. Kurt loved Mirabella. She must not know about this.

That night, when Mirabella began to kiss him, Kurt made sure they made love in the dark. As he moved inside her, he felt the holes he had inserted into the appendage enlarge, the inner line of space spread out. The afternoon's notes were widening.

Through the windows on the surface of the appendage, Kurt felt Mirabella's movement around him as never before. A new awareness of Mirabella – her shape, her form – filled him. He wanted more, something more from her, the definition of which escaped him. Kurt lost himself in space and melody and Mirabella.

Kurt was growing philosophical. He began to watch to determine whether shape moulded space, or space kept shapes apart. He studied Tupperware, margarine containers, water in tea cups.

In this way, Kurt discovered the process of thought. He wondered if meditation, in the Buddhistic mode, dealt with thought as space rather than word. He remembered Mirabella had once said art portrayed thought as shape. She had gone on to say that the female psyche differed from the male in the way it conceived and nurtured identity within space. This, she had stated, was a psychological side effect of the biological womb.

Kurt had laughed, then. Now, he was not so sure. He

was beginning to enjoy his experimentation with the detachable appendage. Still, he hoped this psychic restructuring, this creation of inner space, would not interact with his biological identity to too great an extent. He did not want to get pregnant.

Even with all the psychic structural leaps Kurt was making, the appendage did not detach itself again for months. Kurt had learned to cope with the messy urinating process, and always urinated alone. And then, Kurt and Mirabella attended a wedding.

The best man rose to make the toast to the bride. He raised the glass, so that the red wine swirled in a gentle motion. Kurt started, watching the liquid move within form. The appendage detached.

Kurt caught it at his ankle hem with his serviette, before it hit the floor, then slid it into his pocket. He excused himself from helping to clean up, telling Mirabella something unforeseen had come up, or come off, as the case happened to be. He hurried home.

Feeling like an explorer, Kurt pulled the appendage from his pocket. He kept the memory of the potter's hands in mind, carefully shaping the appendage so that the holes were eliminated. It became a receptacle, delicately shaped and fluted. He cupped it in his palm, smiling.

Inside, a world had opened up, generous in boundaries. Kurt went to the wine cupboard, pulled out the Beaujolais Nouveau. He uncorked it and poured slowly into the bowl shaped appendage. Within the round form, the liquid moved in regular rich red movement. A smooth, quiet ocean bellied out, spreading under the arctic sky. Holding the appendage up, Kurt swirled the wine gently. To contain so much . . . Place, he thought. To be between horizons like this.

Mirabella walked in. Startled, Kurt jerked his arm back behind himself, so that the appendage lost the wine. The red liquid splashed all over the kitchen floor.

"Oh my god – are you alright?" cried Mirabella, thinking it was blood.

Kurt was lightly shaking the appendage into shape behind his back. "Yes," he said, smiling. He turned his back and dropped the appendage into his pants, felt it reassert itself in the normal fashion. "Sorry, love," he said, going over to her.

He placed his arms around her. They enclosed Mirabella's body as if the arms themselves had acquired a new awareness of space and shape. "I love you," he said.

Kurt kissed her, opening his mouth and waiting for her tongue, helping his clothing slide off before her hands. Spreading out on the bed, he cupped himself to receive her, felt within this motion, Mirabella – fluid, moving.

Kurt was visited with a strange, momentary vision of himself on the Oprah Winfrey show, discussing his autobiography, which he had entitled *Self Help To Self Space And Other Inner Vaguenesses*. But the appendage did not seemed to like the image of Oprah with her mike, hovering between ocean and sky. It threatened to close down.

Not even under a pseudonym?

Kurt lost Oprah and the thought of future fame under the circles of Mirabella's intent and a sudden surge of ocean current toward sky.

the operation

i would have thought the mere slice of scalpel
through my seven skins, veined as they are
in ideas of icarus, recycling, and nepal,
would have found the galaxies, alive beyond telescopes,
running my veins, each star, minute as firelit mice eyes,
the elbow of the universe, complete and naive.
but blood swells, not the black of the night sky's gullet,
unpredictably red. "the freezing adds adrenalin,"
dr. yakimetz tells me, scrapes again,
through the last layer. now, i think,
he will find my seventh christmas,
pick out the crumpled wrapping paper, take my brother
early. or he will come across my lover's hand,
cupping my breast from the inside, and amputate.
where is that dream of lions, hung invisible in the air,
or the medusa face, waiting behind each friend's smile?
cut, cut – for it lies, deeper than barefoot daisy meadows,
church choir overtones, the smell of my first child.
medusa haunts the shadow of all relationship,
wears each friend's overcoat backward
as she escorts goodbyes down the front walk.

through the slight yellow fat, he cuts out the white lump
and puckers my skin with dissolving thread. i am confused;
i still feel the st. lawrence strong about the castle
built years ago in my gut for thoughts to come home to.
yet i see i am made up of coloured tapioca pudding,
and that all this doctor found of me was the cyst
above my heart.

elma laverty's lost soul

among the crinkling candy wrappers
of after sermon lemon yellow candies
slipping into children's mouths,
in the foyer,
elma laverty's lutheran index finger
waves like a baton
as she conducts her opinions
on reverend christ church's
latest jigsaw piece hooked into
the overall puzzle of god's revelation.
elma is concerned with the reverend's grammar.

the waggledy, double jointed,
thinner than mercy digit
hypnotizes celia the organist.
it has completed various stars of david,
cats-cradles, has reproduced
kurt browning's gold medal free style pattern,
when this too jointed, double jointed
instrument of judgement disengages,
rises, pale and white as an archangel,
leaping and flickering as an archangel's torch,
up, up, past elma laverty's rigid bosom,
the hierarchy, the bureaucracy
of her mouth first, then ears, eyes, nose,
and small petunia bun.
she has lost her soul; it hovers,
flutters, ducks, and sways,
reduced to apparition and myth
and a footnote in next week's bulletin:

your prayers are requested for elma laverty.
no details given.

but elma's soul, without specific limitations
of navy blue paisley printed arthritis and intelligence ...
this frantic digit compresses the town,
the county (largely chicken farmers, the occasional
plumber, politician, commuting yuppie)
and the drive-in theatre stalls,
under its fingerprint. school hours,
it might perch above the high school condom machine,
swoop down, a rabid albino bat,
on intent. it levitates, in basic question mark form,
beside store owners' cash registers,
flipping numbers back towards zero
on GST calculations. hopping about
reverend christ church's tuesday and thursday
sermon scribblings like an anxious paperweight,
it jabs at chaos and possibility;
the reverend is too liberal in use,
allows the intermingling, the interdenomination,
of 'could,' 'should,' and 'would.'

sucking surreptitiously
on her lemon yellow after sermon treats,
elma joins the town dance band,
shaking the tambourine
and the wednesday morning
women's prayer meeting membership.
elma forgets her soul like a used handkerchief,
lets her petunia bun
find full flowering.

the very wrinkled lives of all
the varied waterstons

the very wrinkled lives
of all the varied waterstons
lost their original seams of consciousness
while blowing their noses.
"blow your nose and the inner ear pressure
changes," states mrs. waterston.
she flaps the wind out of her shirt sleeves.
"we check all our thoughts for fingerprints
to send back to original owners,
but ear pressure changes brain pressure
and we are all a figment of our own imaginations,
anyhow. living in the river valley,
people throw all their dead end thoughts
and stood up conclusions over the escarpment.
they get mixed up with the sitcoms
and the cbc. last week jenny got the sniffles
and became the middle east for three days.
the middle east during the time of christ, that is."
she looks piercingly at the sky. "gladiators,
camels, dressing in my housecoat all day long.
kept tripping over sheep. lucky the tornadoes
hit the suburbs."

it all leads to perforated identities
when the weather changes and the rain
drips through "you"/"me,"
clogging up eavestroughs that run
past to present. foggy days,
timmy may not wear his edmonton oilers shirt,

and all waterstons carry hankies
imprinted with maps full of red arrows
pointing "home." still the twins
mix themselves up with the hamsters
and mr. waterston stands at the front door
with a fog horn, until all waterstons
are in.

"excuse me," says mrs. waterston.
"i just heard caroline sniff.
better get her name tag and pin it
to her memory." she sneezes and reflects:
"but the days the twins have a math test,
i pray they'll get a cold. there are advantages
to this syndrome – but just try and iron out
the wrinkle of a dust allergy."

COULD I HAVE MY
BODY BACK NOW, PLEASE?

The first time Diane entered Mr. Kaethler's corrective visual field, she could hear a complicated series of lenses clicking quietly in his eyes. As she stood in the middle of his office, the eyes focussed in on her, adjusted and readjusted, taking on a predatory gleam. Diane had a fleeting vision of the eyes as parts of a high range telescopic rifle and scolded herself silently for her sexist attitude. Still, she remained uncomfortable; the eyes wavered between vague and intense, shifting from wall to window, to slightly below her throat. At her new desk, just outside Mr. Kaethler's office, she had felt relaxed, well-adjusted. She realized she must have crossed some invisible line near the office door; there was the distinct impression she had entered someone else's territory.

Mr. Kaethler casually flipped an index finger at a chair, then turned to gaze out his wall length window. Relieved to discover that her first assigned task was simply to sit down, Diane sat. The chair was uncomfortable, without arm rests, and its stiff back forced her to sit straighter than she would have chosen. Diane liked to place both feet squarely on the floor and allow her back to slip into its natural intellectual slouch, which she had cultivated during her B.A. years.

As she squirmed about in The Indicated Chair, trying to find some comfortable compromise, Mr. Kaethler turned to face her. Diane noted a frown on his face, and wondered if he suffered from indigestion, or haemorrhoids. Picking up her clipboard and pen, she assumed an absorbent expression

Mr. Kaethler began to pace, clearing his throat and shoving both hands into his pockets. A distracted expression on his middle-aged face, he kept shooting sidelong glances in her general direction. Diane began to sense that something was wrong, out of place. She assessed her own appearance quickly – no nylon runs, no mud on her loafers. Her full brown skirt was complacently zipped up, and she had not made the faux pas of tucking it into her underwear at the back. Uneasily, she sat, clutching at her clipboard. She hoped it was haemorrhoids.

Mr. Kaethler's eyes narrowed, intensified further. They shifted, the pupils crawling across the eye sockets, and attached themselves to her right foot. Unnerved, Diane felt the eyes, like hands, travel up her right leg to just below the knee. They then made a quick hooking motion. During this process, Mr. Kaethler did not speak, but continued to pace and repeat the visual gesture in his sidelong fashion.

After this had gone on for several long, silent moments, Mr. Kaethler once again cleared his throat, made a low whining noise as if disappointed, and began to dictate slowly. As Diane had to look at her clipboard to take down the dictation, she was no longer able to keep track of her boss's odd, jerking eyes.

About halfway through the letter, Diane felt her right foot slowly pick itself up and swing itself gracefully through the air so her right leg crossed her left. The right leg settled, the foot swinging itself back and forth in a gentle motion.

She stopped writing, mid sentence, and stared at her foot. It continued swinging, mid air, and there was a smug look to the rounded loafer toe. Diane knew she had made no conscious decision to cross her legs. She looked at Mr. Kaethler, who had fallen silent.

An expression of fulfillment on his face, he continued to gaze out of the wall length window behind his desk. She saw him nod several times. He began dictating again.

Diane wrote quickly to keep up with the enthusiastic speed Mr. Kaethler's voice had acquired. With her legs crossed, she felt off balance, but she did not want to uncross them, because she would look like an idiot, crossing and uncrossing her legs as if she could not make up her mind, or indeed, had no mind to make up, like an early morning bed.

Diane knew she was different from the other office women, who manipulated their way through the day in push-up bras and bodies defined by aerobics. 'Comfortable' was a term she would have chosen to describe her own body, or 'not argumentative.' It was insulated with just enough fat to make it a body for all seasons. Her uniform was a pair of loafers, a loose full skirt, and a live-and-let-live bra.

Diane figured she could cross her legs during dictation to keep Mr. Kaethler happy. After all, she did not want him to develop a permanent facial tic because she ignored his attempts to communicate through subliminal persuasion. If he was too shy to just come out and say what he wanted, she could accommodate this small need. The next time she went into his office to take dictation, she crossed her legs immediately after sitting down. She noted that Mr. Kaethler gave a small, tight smile to the stuffed deer head on his wall.

Diane set her clipboard on her raised knee, wobbling about on the chair. Waiting for Mr. Kaethler to begin dictation, she found herself surrounded by silence. When she looked up, she found the eyes at work again, fine tuning, focussing . . . but not on her feet. They were riveted to her breasts.

Diane was not sure what to do with her own eyes, which felt as if they had swollen to twice their normal size. She tried to pull her eyelids down discretely over gawking pupils, and think.

It was not a situation in which she could share in the activity, in this case the staring procedure, and develop a relationship with the second person by also turning her gaze upon the third object. If it had been her foot, it would have been a simpler matter to join Mr. Kaethler's eyes, but her breasts were on the other side of her chin and nose, and she would have to dig her chin into her collarbone in an awkward manner. Obviously, she could not solve the situation by crossing one breast over the other, as she had done with her legs. What did Mr. Kaethler want, this time?

Diane tried to block Mr. Kaethler's view of her breasts by raising her clipboard, but all he had to do was pace along the wall instead of the window, in order to place her in profile. She could not very well shift in her chair to match his pacing, without looking paranoid, and she could not move her clipboard so that she was holding it as a shield along the right side of her body, because it looked . . . well, obvious. To look obvious was inappropriate to her position. And besides, then she could not take down the words, and then she would not be doing her job, and then she would be fired.

This sort of situation had to be handled by diplomacy or oblivion. As long as Mr. Kaethler said nothing, neither could she. How was she supposed to introduce the subject? "Excuse me, Mr. Kaethler, but do you have something in your eye? My breasts, perhaps?"

Mr. Kaethler began to dictate, and she scribbled, relieved to have something to do. She could feel the eyes, wherever he paced, fixed on her breasts. They poked, they prodded. They cupped the breasts like hands. They fiddled, removing half an inch here and there. He was sculpting them, pinching away fat, giving them a perky, quirky quality.

Mr. Kaethler dictated to her breasts, addressed and readdressed her breasts, told them how much he appreciated their contributions to the firm, and signed them, 'Yours, Sincerely.'

Diane's breasts had never been given so much attention, at least, not with layers of cloth over them. She felt the rest of her body retreat, try to get away from the breasts, disassociate themselves from the two mounds of flesh. When the letter was completed, she pressed the clipboard to her bosom and left the office as quickly as dignity permitted.

Diane endured Mr. Kaethler's perusal of her breasts for the first week, refusing to think about it. That weekend, on the way to the library, her feet turned, unannounced, into the doorway of the lingerie shop. Half an hour later, she emerged with a new bra.

Monday morning, as she attached the front closing, she felt the new bra's structure close in around her, lift and separate her, hike her mammary glands a good three inches closer to her chin. The breasts now had such an assertive demeanor, they made her nervous. The old self-effacing bra hung from her bedroom door handle, looking a little dumbfounded. This bra made her breasts feel alien, like two hard nodules stuck onto her rib cage. Diane put on more eye liner than usual, glopped on mascara, and drew a determined, ruby red smile onto her mouth.

The secretaries flashed a series of neon lips at her as they recognized her progress towards the office image. "You look lovely," they assured her. Mr. Kaethler's legal partners seemed to realize she existed for the first time, as if she had finally materialized behind the desk she had been inhabiting for a week.

As he watched her bra walk in, Mr. Kaethler's face lit up. Her boss's grin fixed to her torso, Diane felt nothing but relief. She decided she had solved the problem. She seated herself in The Indicated Chair, and he began to dictate, striding up and down the room in a vigorous manner, jacket flapping slightly in the wind he created. At first his eyes surveyed the objects in his office – his paintings, the deer head, the antique lamp. Gradually though, Diane felt the eyes descend upon her mammary glands.

Diane was not particularly enjoying the way her push-up bra manœuvred her through doorways, down hallways, into chairs. She was not used to being this shape, and felt as if she was following her breasts around, trying to keep up. Her torso had now acquired such a fashionable, well defined prominence, that the rest of her felt like continually apologizing, as it sagged along, one step behind.

Mr. Kaethler's eyes poked at her shoulders, and she felt them straighten, push against the chair's stiff back. This made her breasts lift up and shove themselves forward in an alarming manner. She found she had to shift her clipboard forward, almost to the knee, in order to see past her now monumental chest. Aware this could become a precedent setting position, Diane bit her lip. Finally, they got to the 'Yours, Sincerely,' and she tucked the clipboard under her arm, about to stand. Mr. Kaethler smiled at her push-up bra.

"You look very appropriate today, Diane," he said. "It's important to take the time to care for ourselves. A good image demonstrates that we care about ourselves."

"Thank you, sir," Diane muttered. She neglected to mention that all the time she had dedicated to her face and underwear that morning had required she skip breakfast. She had killed her rampaging appetite with coffee, and she was now trying to keep her hyperactive skin in place. She sat, waiting for dismissal.

Mr. Kaethler's eyes intensified their grip on her torso. For a moment, Diane felt her breasts tighten. Then, as if they had some inner hook, like a leggo piece, they lifted up slightly and disengaged. The front of her blouse shifted, as if in a small breeze. She watched in horror as her two breasts, still encased in the push-up bra, passed right through her blouse without opening or tearing the fabric. They hovered mid air, in front of her.

Diane tried to speak, but terror had glued her voice somewhere inaccessible. She stared at her body parts, dangling in front of her. When she glanced at her chest, she saw the blouse hanging limply over her ex-bosom. The disengaged breasts were not bleeding; they seemed to have grown skins all around themselves, and cuddled into the bra, looking content.

"Thank you, Diane – you may go." Mr. Kaethler sounded very pleased with the morning's work.

As she slid off the chair, Diane pressed against its back. She was terrified of coming into contact with her disengaged airborne body parts. She fled Mr. Kaethler's office.

It was evening before she could bring herself to check her torso. When she unbuttoned her blouse, she found her chest completely flat, without nipples, and there was no torn flesh, no scarring, no indication the breasts had ever been there at all. She sat on her bed, staring at her mirror.

Could she go to a doctor, say, "Excuse me, sir, but my boss just gave me a surrealistic mastectomy." Should she go to a priest and confess to an apocalyptic vision? Was there the possibility of taking Mr. Kaethler to court? Perhaps she could grab the hovering breasts tomorrow, drag them out of the office and over to a judge as evidence. She lay awake worrying most of the night, and her dreams presented no solutions. Too tired to eat breakfast, she applied the office uniform to her face and straggled off to work.

"Diane – are you on some weight loss program?" a secretary demanded. "You lucky thing, you."

Diane pushed her lipstick into a smile and headed for the coffee machine, hoping for an IQ rush.

With trepidation, she opened the office door, wondering what mood the eyes would be in. She saw Mr. Kaethler at his desk, surveying her dictation chair over his church steeple hands, something near a smile on his mouth. She followed the line of his gaze and gasped. There were her two breasts, still in the push-up bra, hovering just in front of her chair.

"Come in and sit down, Diane," Mr. Kaethler murmured.

Diane slid onto her chair, keeping a close eye on the breasts and bra. She defended herself with her clipboard, preparing to strike out at them if they made any sudden moves. For a moment, the body parts floated demurely, then, without so much as an "Excuse me," or "Do you mind if . . . ?" they slipped silently through the clipboard and blouse and attached themselves to her chest. Her clipboard moved out and was leaning against them, in normal, moral fashion.

For a second, Diane wondered if she should switch to decaffeinated coffee. She flipped the clipboard against her bosom, and found it solid enough. She decided to ignore the whole incident, try to act professional, and get on with the dictation.

After Mr. Kaethler dismissed her, the breasts and bra again detached themselves, hovering just out of reach. He was observing her, but his attention had dropped about a foot lower than usual. The door looked a long way off. Diane turned and walked as quickly as was appropriate.

There was a prodding sensation at her right buttock, then the left. She was being assessed, measured. Diane moaned – the door seemed to be retreating. In panic, the muscles along her lower back, buttocks and upper thighs tightened, clamping everything into place. Two feet from the door, she felt first the right, then the left buttock, disengage slowly and slide through the back of her skirt. Suddenly two sizes too large, her underwear and nylons began to slide down her legs. Diane grabbed at her underwear and whirled around. The two pale curves of flesh hung, waist high, in front of her. Mr. Kaethler watched them, smiling.

In spite of his presence, Diane let go of her underwear and made a grab at the hovering buttocks. It was her bum, after all, and she wanted it – needed it, even. She saw her hand swing through the air, then pass right through the buttocks. Though in shock, she kept enough presence of mind to grab at her rapidly descending underwear and nylons, hauling them back up. She ran out the door.

When she sat down at her desk, she found her bum had gone flat, so that her pelvis rubbed against the chair's wooden surface. She borrowed three sweaters, and sat on them. When she observed herself in the mirror that night, she had become a straight line, shoulder to hip. With the weight she had been losing lately due to her new caffeine diet, she was almost a stick.

"Diane, you devil – you are losing weight!" the secretaries complained the next day. "How are you getting away with this so fast?"

"I think it's getting away from me," Diane mumbled. She shuffled to the coffee machine for breakfast.

At the next dictation session, Diane walked in to discover her buttocks and breasts anxiously hovering around her dictation chair. What made them appealing to Mr. Kaethler? Diane wondered. Why would he want to hold them hostage in this way? Disconnected like that they resembled uncooked dough, or bizarre bumblebees. As she approached, they perked up, zoomed in on her, and attached themselves. Diane sighed and sat down.

"Good to see you looking so well," Mr. Kaethler commented. "You're beginning to really fit in here – more and more appropriate for our office image, Diane."

Diane looked at him. She almost said, "Could I have my body back now, please?"

Today, Mr. Kaethler dictated to her crotch. When she stood up to leave, Diane closed her eyes. She did not want to see what would disengage. Sometimes, ignorance was bliss ... at least temporarily.

That evening, her pubic hair was gone.

The next day, the eyes moved in on her long blond hair, stroking, caressing, pulling it from her head. Next it was her make-up, carefully lifted off so that eye liner, mascara and shadow floated vacantly above an outline of ruby red lips. Off to one side of her head, her earrings bobbed, reluctant to separate. Diane noted this with sympathy. Stick together, ladies, she silently advised.

"Diane, you get younger every day!" the other secretaries exclaimed. "You could be a model!"

With her short hair and pre-pubescent body, Diane was

beginning to feel, in Mr. Kaethler's presence, like an early adolescent. She burst into tears in an erratic fashion while taking dictation, and Mr. Kaethler was admirably understanding, patting her shoulder and awkwardly handing her kleenex.

Diane dreaded the voice that summoned her to dictation, dreaded the moment she walked through the door to be confronted by this drifting constellation of body parts. Sometimes, Mr. Kaethler silently refused to allow the parts to attach, kept them floating about her while she took dictation, so that they made her feel dizzy. Then it became difficult to concentrate. The days he allowed the parts to slide onto her body as soon as she walked through the door were a relief.

Then came a day when Mr. Kaethler used the word 'appropriate' once too often. With a start, Diane realized that 'appropriate' was not only an adjective, it was a verb.

"Appropriate, appropriate," she muttered, scribbling it several times on her clipboard. "Look this up," she wrote beside it, then asked Mr. Kaethler to repeat his last sentence. He frowned, scolding her for letting her mind drift. She wanted to say, "Sorry sir, but there's a bum in my face," but opted for a better part of valour. Where had this attitude come from? She had not wanted to laugh since her first week on this job.

"Appropriate: adjective – suitable to a particular person, thing, or situation," read her dictionary. "Appropriate: verb – take for oneself; assign possession of; annex; assign to a special purpose."

"Diane, you look so appropriate," Diane muttered, feeling brilliant. "Diane, I appropriate you, today."

Diane found thinking gave her an enormous appetite – one that could not be abated by the variety of canned soups she had been accumulating in her cupboards over the past few months. She cooked herself a meal of fish, potatoes and two vegetables, and with the energy rush that trailed the digestive process, she sat and pondered.

She found she enjoyed re-acquainting herself with her mind, and in the morning, munched her way through toast, cereal, and orange juice. When she arrived at the office, she allowed herself one cup of coffee. As she walked into Mr. Kaethler's office to take dictation, she felt her thoughts lean forward to observe Mr. Kaethler, an aura of anticipation draped over them.

Dinner and breakfast seemed to have settled onto her. She was aware of every bone in her body – the skull, vertebrae, pelvis, arms, and leg bones. She felt the muscles entwine and grip the bone. She knew the mass and weight of each organ, felt the myriad of tunnels her blood sped through. Everything was solid, real, and holding onto everything else like a United Way campaign.

When she approached The Indicated Chair with its thin back and seat, its four narrow legs, the piece of furniture looked flimsy, unable to support this recently acquired awareness of the massive interconnection of blood and bone, brain and beating heart.

Looking around, her eyes focussed on another chair – a black leather armchair, its back to the wall. It looked as if it bench-pressed bull elephants for a hobby. Diane sat down in it, splayed her arms out over the arm rests, and caressed the floor with the bottoms of both feet. She surveyed Mr. Kaethler.

Mr. Kaethler, who had been leaning back in his chair, watching her floating body parts, straightened. His face appeared confused. For the first time, he looked Diane in the eye. Her voice was so calm, it dropped several pitches below its regular tone. "Good morning, Mr. Kaethler. How are you today?"

She saw the eyes shift away. They looked vague, unfocussed. "Fine, fine," he mumbled uneasily.

"Well," Diane said. "Why don't we begin?"

Her voice sounded odd in this room. Her quota of syllables per dictation session had hovered around five. Caught up in a burgeoning recklessness, she forged ahead.

"So what is it that you would like me to take down today sir?" asked Diane. The constellation of body parts circling around her dictation chair perked up and swivelled in her direction.

Mr. Kaethler appeared to have been attacked by memory loss. "Give me a minute. Give me a minute," he mumbled. He stood up and looked out the window, clasping his hands behind his back so that Diane had a good view of them. One of the fingers began jerking, pointing from Diane to The Indicated Chair. It repeated the gesture, at first slowly, then frantically. Diane smiled, and let the silence stretch itself out and yawn.

Then she said, "Sir, I really do have a lot of work to process – end of the month, and all. I'd appreciate it if we could complete the letter quickly."

Mr. Kaethler's finger stopped jerking back and forth. He cleared his throat and began the letter, pacing in front of his desk.

Now that she was sitting with her back to the wall, Mr. Kaethler could not walk behind her. Diane found she was able to concentrate on more than getting down the words; she had time and energy to absorb the content of the sentences as she took them down. She ignored the body parts, which Mr. Kaethler had trailing after him in a long, obedient line. She asked questions to clarify content, she corrected grammar, and once offered an alternative for a choice of word.

Each time she did this, the body parts would drift out of line behind Mr. Kaethler's back and turn in her direction. They scooted back quickly whenever he shot a corrective glare in their direction. Finally, the letter was complete, and Mr. Kaethler said, staring out the window, "You are dismissed, now, Diane."

Diane stood, tucked the clipboard under her arm, and said cheerfully, "And thank you for your time, Mr. Kaethler." She took note as the body parts took a collective surge towards her, winked at them, and left the room.

Over the next few days, Diane continued to sit in the black leather chair. She paraded her voice around the room, enjoying its presence. One morning, after a particularly invigorating breakfast of oatmeal and bran muffins, she advised Mr. Kaethler as to the rumpling of his tie, and the askew nature of his toupee.

The more she talked, the less Mr. Kaethler paced. He began to stand behind his desk, staring out the window, keeping her body parts perched beside him on the windowsill. As an experiment, Diane got up out of the chair, and began to meander about the room, scribbling as she went.

The body parts scampered towards her like curious kittens, breasts and buttocks bulging with effort. Mr. Kaethler's back stiffened. He turned and surveyed the office for a floating buttock, breast, or earring, but they had all scooted in behind Diane's now sturdy, solid body. Diane heard the lenses clicking in Mr. Kaethler's eyes. He sent his gaze flicking over everything in the office but Diane herself. Her form, he gave a visual buffer zone of six inches all around.

Must be my aura, Diane grinned to herself.

As she paced, the parts scurried along beside her, keeping out of Mr. Kaethler's visual field. "Let me read this letter back to you," Diane suggested, and began to proclaim the words as Moses must have announced the Ten Commandments; she was feeling very important.

Mr. Kaethler wilted under the sound of her voice, which rolled through the stale office air, syllable building onto syllable. He sat down, swivelled the chair so he could look out the window, and crawled down between his shoulders.

First the buttocks hooked themselves back on, then the breasts in the bra. Soon the air was empty of floating pubic hair, jewelry, make-up, and long blond hair.

"Would you like that signed 'Yours, Sincerely,' or

'Sincerely, Yours'?" Diane asked thoughtfully.

Mr. Kaethler whispered, "You decide, Diane. I'm sure you can think of something appropriate."

"I'll certainly put my mind to it," Diane assured him cheerfully. She heard her thoughts chuckle. "Anything else you needed looking after?"

There was a pause. Then, "God, no," Mr. Kaethler said feebly.

Diane felt her eyes focus on the toupee and slide under it like spatula shaped lasers. The toupee lifted slightly. Power surged through her like a line drawn tight. For a moment, she was tempted, hesitated. Mr. Kaethler did not move.

Then Diane blinked several times, and shifted her gaze to the ceiling. Remember this, Mr. Kaethler, she thought at him grimly. I am leaving you with yours.

She turned and left the office, taking all of herself with her.

helen

not of troy.
of churchill, manitoba.

born fisted, of another, helen's smile explains.
girls at this winnipeg treatment centre
come from under
drugs, memory, alcohol, men,
us,
carry rage like a fetus
curled into hands, shoulders, balls
of feet; they nurse their walk.
social workers watch the womb
of their eyes,
are here to abort.

helen of the black hair,
the wide brown skin, wider than attitudes:
'dysfunctional,' 'psychotic,' 'emotional-
ly disturbed' . . . 'schizophrenic.'
around her, battles walk, soft footed,
white faced warriors fight with pills
and degrees of psychology, sociology,
tell her she belongs within
this civilization of definitions they build
to house her.

her bones are hands, open palmed,
display her like a banner, like sky;
inside a horizon, wider than her need
to breathe . . . how does this girl?

memory tracks her, unfolds like sleep,
the sky can crumple like a fist –
try to breathe . . . how does this girl?
wire run through her
third storey bedroom window
in the winnipeg treatment centre, bars across
her eyes, helen watches.

and this rage, it gains a heart,
begins to see. the fingernails grow,
and the voice. we must abort,
we must abort; it is a child
of the wrong experience; it cannot be allowed
to exist. helen must learn to kill
(it is only a matter of words,
of culture)
herself.

time within eyes, helen watches.
social worker explains in words
the way a wrist watch assumes
it measures the width, the weight of sun,
but time is a dealer,
pulls moments like cards
from its deck.
the space within the atom pulls apart,
yesterday widens in her joints,
limbs do not connect.
where do the faces she cut
and pasted to the present go?

tangents are opportunities,
sudden new landscapes;
helen begins laughter as a journey
in broad, disappearing footfalls,
returns when she is ready
from the better places.

social worker scrubs her own white skin,
seeks to wash away the myth,
the helen . . . of churchill, manitoba,
closed into this winnipeg treatment centre;
social worker wants to believe the words –
this is merely a problem of juxtaposition;
two cultures overlap, do not observe
the dead line, outline, somewhere
someone drew around us.

contain helen. teach her
to speak. she will fit
into your womb.

(marie's) phantom limb

eyes, two potholes, gouged out by dreams
that spin without forward momentum,
tearing treadmarks into (marie's face),
others found above a girl's neck
blue with fingerprints
(not red as the vortex
torn below her womb).

and now (she is) closed in
by mesh enforced plexiglass,
fluorescent lighting.
(marie) rocks (her) body
about the old teddy bear
(nobody knows (she) keeps meds
in cheeks like cherry pits.
shoves them up the toy's ass),
watching the sun stain a constipated sky,
seep into bloated skyscraper windows –
eyes of buildings dyed.

the therapist has eyes in his ears,
watching for (her) words.
"talk is our cure," he muses –
"(your past marie is)
a phantom limb.
with our words
(you will) remember,
see this missing limb,
learn to walk again."

(she) turns to look into the past;
it is a mirror empty of reflection –
the phantom is (her) face,
not (her) leg.
(she) spins careful, intricate
patterns of silence,
catches therapeutic words that buzz
in thick afternoon sunlight.
no one moves but the dust.

then force without definition;
the vortex looms – (she is)
defaced in wordless screams,
a sharpened pencil each stroke dulls
and when (she is) tired, empty,
there are no words,
only the lead stump,
and the throb in a body
(marie does not see)
with its missing limb as modern art –
perhaps the odd whim
of a divine cartooner holidaying
in lethbridge, or greece.

"talk to me, (marie),"
say the staff with pills in their hands;
they push hours ahead of them,
their shoulders curved against
invisible boulders.
they record (her) actions on 'daily logs;'
(she) records (her) present
with mirror fragments against
(her) wrists – phantom wrists;
(she) records (her) present
against (her) past;
only the pain (is real).

(marie waits for)
a time untroubled by dreams.
at night the wind
steals tiny children's faces
and blows them about like confetti;
in gutter puddles they lose their features.
(marie) scoops them into (her) hands,
sorts them to colours.
with the pocket mirror's empty eye
(she) uses them to form (herself)
a new face of dreams
(she) then wears
into terrors of day.

DUST IN THE LIGHT

The warm afternoon sun lapped, fluid, against Mel's toes. Outside the window, the back yard swirled and dimpled; today, the wind had playful fingers. Cautiously, Mel moved her head half an inch. This new angle superimposed the small round fault in the window glass over a top hinge in Mindy's old swing set, giving the rusting metal joint an awkward bulge. The glass knot hovered like a pebble just dropped into water, its impact beginning to send out circles.

She was watching the dust float in the window light. Fingerprinted by the sun, each speck drifted in slow currents of air. Suddenly, Mel sat up and smashed her left arm, like an iron beam, through the complacent dust. The specks whirled about, dashing into one another. Intent, she stared, heart beating in excitement, as anguished specks were wrenched from their ebb and flow. Uncertainly, the dust settled, began to drift. Mel sat back, moving the rocker gently. She waited.

There was something – some idea, or memory, that crouched beneath the thin verbal surface of her thought. She could not define it by shape or colour, but she knew it was there. It was small, hard, and it irritated her. Mel frowned, swung her left arm through the light, and watched in disgust as the dust panicked, then resided.

The elbow joint, the place her left arm ended, was clear to her. They, Dave and Rachel, kept saying, kept insisting her forearm was there, but she knew it was not. She could feel the void after the scar, the space where that endless flow of dust and air began.

The light coagulated into a puddle on the hardwood floor, swelled between her toes. There was a book in her right hand, open to page seventy-eight, but her mind floated, having lost its line to a tenuous plot. The warm lip of the sun washed up against her feet and receded; she could hear it scrape and shift against the wooden floor.

Of course she was conscientious about the missing arm. She had learned to work with the right, and held her upper left arm carefully against her side, had worked to adjust to the unbalanced state of her body. This was why she preferred the rocker. It was like sitting within two arms, cradled in a perfect resting motion.

There was never any warning. The wild jerk came at her from inside, and she was dragged feet first into memory. The storm rose, fists in the sky, blotting out the sun. Water heaved, black. Then the wave shoved up and over the gunwale in a great, grey hand. As the two of them began to slide across the deck, Mel felt Mindy leave the inside of her arm.

She grabbed her daughter's hand with both her own. Later, she had counted the small tears the girl's fingernails left on the skin of her right hand, refused, for the first few months, to let them heal, gently reopening them. She had needed the reminders – the four small scabs.

She did not see the little girl go over. Mel was slammed against the gunwale, her face held down by water. She had to take one hand away – to grab onto the boat. She held onto her daughter with the other.

The psychiatrist kept reassuring her that she had made the correct choice. To have maintained a grip on Mindy with both hands would have proven fatal for both of them. But Mel remembered how her right hand had gripped the gunwale – there had been no doubt about the connection.

The psychiatrist said the boat had been easier to hold onto, because it had strong, moulded edges, unlike fingers.

This was her last sight of Mindy's face – the small pale

blur around the open mouth. In this memory, Mel could find no emotion. She had to work to hang on – to the boat, to her daughter's slipping hand. Her hands gripped, they clamped down. She had bones and muscles with the intensity of steel.

There was no energy left for emotion.

The psychiatrist insinuated this was a function of denial, but Mel knew better. Had he ever visited her memory? There was only the cold, solid wind, the boat's swinging up, and then the heavy, metal bar that came crashing down across her left elbow, cutting it off like a knife.

She had waited for the mention of her left forearm, the fingers wrapped like wire around her daughter's hand. When, two days later, they had brought the news of the body washed ashore, there had been no description of the grip still attached to the swollen hand. There had been no news of it.

She wondered where it had gone, if the arm had been eaten by otters, or a stray dog. There was always this question, in delicate specks that shifted about her brain.

Mel drifted back to her body, to the book in her right hand, to the cushion sliding out from under her on the rocker's wooden seat. She set the book on the floor, stood, and rearranged the cushion with her right hand. As she sat, she noted the way the dust whirled in the sunlit currents caused by her movement.

It was a while back now – Mel could not remember exactly how long – that her husband and daughter had moved behind glass, the sort of glass with a wave effect. When Dave or Rachel shifted, faults in the glass caused their faces and bodies to ripple, as if underwater. She wondered, sometimes, how they breathed, how they got at air. She had stopped trying to get at the words she knew were leaving their mouths in dark bubbles of sound. They rarely broke the transparent, vacillating surface.

Mel had been the one to tie the tourniquet above the elbow, using her teeth and her right hand. She was not sure she had gotten it tight enough to stop the glow of blood spurting out, staining the air, her clothing, the deck. Dave had tried to stop her. She had had to shove him away, thinking him mad with grief, wanting them all to die. One was enough.

She went to the psychiatrist to please him. Dave had attended three sessions, to get her started. She realized this in retrospect; at first she had thought they were in it together.

The psychiatrist's strange insinuations irritated her. This must have been about the time – those first sessions – that she felt the others shift to profile, begin to talk at her from strange angles. She had watched as the psychiatrist promoted Dave to co-worker, and she became their mutual patient. The distance stretched out between them, as thin, as hard, as faulty, as glass.

She began to take the anti-depressants to get them off her back, and after the first few blood tests, they stopped checking to ensure she was swallowing, on a regular basis, their perspective. When she had their confidence, tight in the sweaty palm of her own confidence, Mel dropped the pills down the vent. She had learned how the pills spoke her words. She could imitate well enough.

Mel tried it again. She had insisted Rachel cut all of her left sleeves short so that the hems dangled just below the left elbow. Now, as Mel pulled the hem up, she could see the place where the forearm had been torn from her body, from the clutch of the elbow joint. The hospital still refused to operate, to patch over the area and make it more attractive. It had healed unevenly, and remained, a purple cloud on her skin.

When she held her left arm up and out, the two inches above the elbow were cradled by sunlight. Palm against palm, heat nudged scar.

She reconstructed the reality of Mindy's hand – the way the soft flesh ridged the inside of the upper palm, the way it dimpled and gave way to pressure. She felt the warm hollow, the soft heels of their hands, the way the little hand sweated in hers. As Mel walked her youngest daughter to the red brick school on the corner, there was the tight circle of their two hands, a small, complete circle, their fingers going round and round so tightly, the space between their hands became suction, pulling the hands closer together.

The jerk came again. Mel's head went back; she bumped against the rocker, trying to pull out of memory. But the rocker swung forward; her chest slammed against gunwale. After, her breasts and upper left arm had been one dark bruise. She was trying to get air in around the water that filled her mouth and nose.

They said in a plane crash, the parent was to put on the oxygen mask, then adjust the child's.

There was no room, no time, for fear, for terror. There was Mindy's face, mouth open, the small dark circle a tiny fingerprint of unheard sound. Mel could not hear Mindy's voice. There was not even the roar of the metal bar as it came down.

The scene twisted, faded like a bruise. Body pushed against the rails of the rocker, feet shoved floor. Small sun eddies had seeped up to her knees. Mel stared at the point her arm ended, her need to breathe pushing like two small palms against the inside of her chest.

They said her arm was there.

At first, she thought they had gone crazy in their grief. Face blotched and puffy, for weeks Rachel's eyes looked as if someone had gotten at them with the fine edge of glass. Mel did not trust those eyes. They could not be trusted to see a missing arm.

Dave, too, had wept constantly. He had wanted to talk about Mindy – talk about her face, her voice, her hands. Mindy had loved her own hands, had talked with them. They had been like small summer insects, floating about her face.

Mel had not been able to locate where grief huddled in her body. Initially, she thought it might have been washed away by the storm; later, she decided it had frozen somewhere below her stomach. She developed an image of herself, frozen solid from neck to waist, and below this, she saw a chainsaw running, steady, in her gut. She knew it was doing damage, did not need a psychiatrist to tell her it needed to be dealt with, but the ice in between had shut down her connection to the pain. Someday, she supposed, the ice would melt. Someday was some other day.

She felt nothing. Her body, her face, her skin, were like cellophane, stretched thin and transparent. Too much movement, and a small tear would let her out, sheer, cold, and relentless. There would be no feeling to it; it would be unstoppable as the storm pouring in over the deck.

Mel let the air in – small breaths, testing her lungs. She lifted her arm again, into the edge of the sun. The warmth moved up from her left elbow – two small hands, patting uncertainly. Mel imagined her arm there, between the gold dust specks. She imagined the small points of light lengthening, becoming the hairs on her arm, the short fine lines of gold.

Due to their fragile appearance, Mel had always surprised others with the strength of her arms. She imagined intricate patterns of wire inside her skin, steel bones, details of nuts and bolts at her joints. She did not allow herself the fragility of human flesh, its unguaranteed status.

She did not have to accept that. She refused it. Always, her arms held her own to her body. They had never failed her.

The psychiatrist kept wanting to talk about Mindy. "You've got to face the fact she's dead," he would pronounce. "You've got to let go of her."

Mel thought this nonsense. Of course her daughter was dead. Did they think she was stupid? Just because the man had a degree, he thought he could see the thoughts shifting about in her brain before they consolidated to words. How could this god damn psychiatrist talk about what happened in her head, it being a place he had never been? And would never be, if she had any choice about it.

Mel would sit in that office, watch the psychiatrist watch her – he, on the other side of glass he did not even know existed. Glass muffled his words.

Mindy rested in the curve of Mel's left arm, the dark wiry curls poking at her upper arm. The lamp's light settled into her hair, vibrant, demanding. Her hand a copycat gesture of Mel's, Mindy followed her habit of settling her small left arm over the curve of her mother's. They had read all of *The Velveteen Rabbit* in this position.

She could see where the elbow joint ended. When she moved her right hand into the sun, it became pale, white – a ghost. Why did it pretend to grasp at life, why did it not give up and disappear, as the other had done? She passed her right hand through the air, just below the left elbow. Nothing – there was nothing there.

When she concentrated on imagining her left forearm, it took on the chicken drumstick shape, covered in random brown freckles. The wrist almost collapsed in on itself, bones pushing up like wings against the skin. There were the blue veins arching through the hand, the demands of the bones casting shadows, the ridge of knuckles, their release into fingers.

There were times when Mel focussed herself completely onto this space. For an instant, the dust would falter, realign, take on the temporary shape of an arm, or a shadow, projected by memory.

I am good at holding things, Mel thought. I have the grip of a steel pincer.

She had thought of her hands as her strongest part, stronger than her heart. She remembered watching them at work, like colleagues, cutting fruit, typing essays, knitting spare moments to permanent shapes and memories. They had been her most admirable part, the place where skin and bone became machine.

She imagined her left hand, turned so that it cupped the warm light in its palm. She imagined the thumb moving outward, the pale fingers spreading out into water, the light filtering between, warming edges. Hesitation held her breath. The fingers looked fragile, thin.

This time, she imagined the light, its warmth creating shadow and light on the ridges of the skin, in among the fingerprints, spilling over the heel of her hand, down along the wrist, through the blue of the veins.

Again, memory came at her, snatched her feet from under her, tore left hand from right. Her right hand latched onto the gunwale, strong. The shape of the metal bar slammed down across the thin white line of arm, cutting off Mindy's face.

On the other side of the window, orange, red, and yellows lapped at edges of leaves. This meant a breeze, and the full, wet smells of autumn. Outside, there would be the rustling of leaves, a bend in the grass. In here, the clock ticked; there was the hum of the fridge. If she moved, she could cause a creak in the rocker's rails.

She remembered a jar of peaches, splintering to a confetti of glass and amber on the kitchen floor. The rough metal lid rasped against her fingers.

She remembered Rachel's cheekbone, pressed in a long, hard moment against her left palm, the echo of the slap.

This time, fear rushed at her, sky wide. She saw it twist the water into a series of black hands that slapped at their boat. Panic unclenched in her gut, whirled outward. The boat swung wildly.

Dave caught at Rachel, shoved her towards the cabin. Turning, Mel saw Mindy at the other end of the boat, black hair whipping about her face. Mel struggled to reach her. Underneath, the deck heaved and wretched. Panic wedged up through her chest, between her joints. Bones separated, drifted like steel girders as their screws slid out. She fell against the deck.

But she had her – Mel had her daughter's hand. She twisted her legs around the small bench bolted to the deck and hung on. The wave came, bigger than anything Mel had ever imagined. It was black, solid. Her hands gripped Mindy. Then the wave, with a dream's ease, unhooked her legs from the bench, and slammed her up against the side of the boat.

She still had Mindy's hand, felt the water pick the girl up and move her over the gunwale. The small fingers, wet, cold, were hooked through her own.

The gunwale rammed in against her, entering her chest, cutting off her air, her fear, terror. Mel sent out everything she had, still alive, still moving in her body, down along that left arm, into the bone and muscle, and held onto the small fingers. Her left elbow lifted and smashed down against the boat. Mindy's face bobbed, blurred in the water, dark hair pressed flat across her forehead, into the small black space of her mouth.

She could see the small fingers now, twisted between her own. They were cold, wet. They were like small worms, sliding out of her own fingers.

The silence in her mind melted. Mel heard the scream that had frozen into the black circle of Mindy's mouth. She could not have heard it in the storm, but she heard it now. It plummeted through her ears, down through her gut, disappeared into a deeper quiet.

The face faded into black water. The fingers left. Her own hand, her disappointed flesh, stretched out, ghost of its own intent, out into water and wind.

The fault in the window pane, the small knot, had been absorbed into the glass. The sun now held her completely in its palm. Heat rippled against her abdomen. Slowly, Mel took her right index finger and traced the flesh of her left forearm, the freckles, the fine gold hairs, the fingers that cupped their empty handful of light.

six month environmentalist

six month marcus
is back porch absorbing
black butterflies skydancing.
it is the maple tree,
leaves wind hung
and whispering,
fluttering the sun.

no dimensions, distance.
the floating leaves, shadowskin,
flicker – lily pads underskin.
thought, heart beat . . .
wind cob web tracing
across nose.

he shrieks, warbles;
cool space, each leaf
fingerprints warm sun.

moody wind
crawls around a corner
and leaves die across eyes,
become like roses in wallpaper –
but the wallpaper never moved.
marcus's face, eyes become still,
his voice, like a door closed.
heart beat climbing stairs
grows tired, cannot find
the next step.

marcus explodes to wail.
two hands must lift, move, hold
him close to warm moving skin.
he feels heart beat of
someone, another,
knows this is,
goes on.

child dreamwalks sky

the morning moon over the hydro wire
half a footprint
between curtains
of a pregnant wind.
magpie trickles across window,
condenses onto first floor
mountain ash.

I hear the tattered laugh
of the downstairs vietnamese child.
she is an ocean builder;
i have seen the currents
in her eyes.
she tells me
stonehenge was set up
so the gods could play dominoes.
this child sews her dreams
into the hem of her skirt.
i watch her brilliant pirouette
on the september lawn,
feel the edge of night
brush my face
in the trembling curtain lace.

i wonder if the child
sees the moon fade,
if she knows the piece of sky
she tucked carefully into her shoe
will not carry her
out of her pirouette?
in another window, mother
calls daughter from her kaleidoscope –
colour, shape is relative
and time stretches, curls around
in tight, wild circles.

in the dew,
dreamer's footprints drift
out of their circle,
lose toe hold on sky;
day is the sun's walking place.

but there are half moons
hovering in my curtains.
the wind remembers.

the first gods

I

childhood has that extra stab
of colour.
perhaps because the shapes
live higher up
they catch more of the sun.
purples are more purple,
reds more red.
there is a line on the sofa
drawn by the fingertip
of the high bright sun;
it divides the lighter
from the darker.
you know the moments
when the sun dips down
into your world.
the air becomes a warm velvet.
the dust that dances about you
is lit to small yellow stars.
but then the sun
picks up her feet.
you know she has somewhere
to go
for she pulls back the warm palm
you were sitting on
and leaves you with cold linoleum,
hardwood floor, the darkness
under the tablecloth.

II

faces are hard to talk to.
they move slightly lower
than the sun,
wear ceilings and chandeliers
as very large hats.
suddenly they will swoop
down from the world that moves
above your head.
those mountainpeak sounds
zoom sharply into focus
three inches from your face.
you feel the voices change
as they enter a world
below their wallets.
they are as soft as flannel:
aren't you cute?
say hi to auntie.

III

you know the big people
by the bottoms of their voices –
aunties blue and pink knit slippers
with their soft balls you try
to catch hold of
with your fingers,
father's rough brown sox –
at one end a smooth pink bump
sticks out.
it is the only small thing
of the big people
you can see;
it is the size
of your hand.
those big feet –

always in twos,
always moving,
they carry the voices with them.
you hear them somewhere
on the edge of your ears.
then they bring the feet in,
the pant legs
or skirt hem.
sometimes they move
through your eyes,
ruffle the air that drowses
about you like a blanket.
the feet are gone
and the air settles.
somewhere in a corner
of your ear
the voices carry on.

IV
and then the voices bring hands.
they are warmer
than sleeping air,
stronger,
take you up
to the world of faces
closest the sun's one eye.

ANSWERS

Linden liked to listen. When she was very little, her mother said her ears were shaped like two small question marks. With every sound, Linden seemed to have a question. Why does the fridge burp? Why does the kitchen floor crack its knuckles? Why do frying onions sound like a river? Why can I hear more than one sound at a time?

That last question, Linden's mother decided, was a very good one. Her son was only able to hear his walkman. She could not figure out why her daughter had to turn the world into such a complicated bundle of noises. Shaking her head, Linden's mother turned up Julio Iglesias, and sang, "To All The Girls I Have Loved" into her wooden spoon.

Every now and then, Linden came up with her own answers. She discovered what kinds of shoes the sky wore. She knew the hail wore tap dance shoes. The rain sometimes kicked at her window with heavy snowboots. On days of light spring rain, the drops jumped around on ballet toes. Then the sun came out, tiptoeing down the green stalks of grass so as not to get its Chinese slippers wet. There were the hot humid Ontario afternoons, when the sun stomped on her skin in Dutch wooden shoes. She thought she could hear her skin crackle with heat. Long into the night, she felt the hot invisible heel marks and she listened to her forearms and cheeks grumble.

Linden taught herself to fall asleep by listening to the moon. She knew it wore a long white dress and made a soft silver sound. If she listened to it carefully, she could hear the moon walk slowly up the dark stairway into the night sky. Her long white dress stretched behind her, far into other countries. Linden's mother had told her that countries had night at different times. Linden decided that the moon walked from country to country, checking to make sure all the eyelids were closed. Her dress was so long, it stretched from one country back into the morning hours of the country before it. There must be a stairway, Linden decided, that stretched all the way around the world, and the moon was kept very busy climbing the stairs. Someone else was also kept busy sweeping off the stairs, for the moon's dress was always very clean and white.

In the winter time, the moon climbed into the sky earlier. Before supper time, Linden would watch her, and if the tv was not on, she would listen for tiny footsteps among the stars. Later, when she climbed into bed between the flannel sheets, she shivered and shivered all her body heat into the sheets until she had made a warm cave for herself. Then she would lie still, with her eyelids closed, and listen.

There it would come, that soft silver sound of it – the low swish of the moon's white robe as the hem flowed over her windowsill. It came across her floor, up over her bed, across her eyelids and down into the dark wooden panelled hallways of her mind. That silver sound brought with it a silver light that filled the rooms in her head. Once the moon lit up her dreams, Linden was not afraid. She would smile and go to sleep.

It was just after Linden's fourth birthday, that her ears began to grow. Of course they had been growing all along, just like her nostrils and fingerprints. After her fourth birthday, they began to grow differently. When Linden listened especially closely to something, her ears began to grow. As long as she listened, they kept growing. Sometimes they took on the shape of the sound's keeper. In the long summer evenings at their cottage, the loon's cry would flit across the lake's surface, among the dreaming trees. Almost as a reflection, Linden's ears took on the slender fluted shape of a loon's head. At the zoo, her ears imitated shapes of growls, whimpers and grunts, then shrunk to a pencil dot outside the cage of the soldier ants. Finally, they took wing beside the great horned owl.

Adults found it disconcerting to see themselves silhouetted on Linden's ears. Linden's mother quickly learned to stop waving her arms and wooden spoon. She did not like the white pasty shapes that grew out of her daughter's head, scowling back at her. She made Linden wear her hair long, hoping this would conceal the defective quirk her daughter seemed to be cultivating.

Linden alone was not alarmed at this new development. She was not yet in kindergarten and did not know many children her own age. She did not feel anything when her ears grew or changed shape. There was only one disadvantage that she had spotted.

One evening, she stood outside the kitchen door, listening in on her parents' conversation. She knew they were discussing her upcoming appointment with the family doctor, and she had heard a comment about her ears. Since the conversation was about her, Linden wanted to hear it. She stood close to the door, and listened.

She concentrated hard to hear the words – syllables that bowed quickly on stage, like marionettes, then slipped out through the big velvet curtain. Suddenly an oversound began to slam a door in regular rhythm, copied by its little echo. It was her heart, picking itself up and throwing itself against her chest as if it were the surface of a big bass drum. She could hardly hear her parents speaking. She listened closer.

Linden did not notice as her ears extended into long white ribbons. They crept down the door's surface until they reached the floor, then slid underneath. As they grew up the door's other side, one took on her mother's shape. The other took on her father's. Her mother was waving her arms.

"Sensitive, yes," said her mother, "but she's weird.

What's the good of sensitive, when everyone's going to laugh at her? They'll say it's a congenital defect. Maybe we could get the doctor to cut off her ears, and sew on somebody else's."

Then her mother spotted Linden's ears. She stared at them in silence. At first Linden was confused by this lack of sound. She frowned, staring harder through the key hole. The small hole hovered at her eye level, and she could not see her parents' faces, or their crossed arms. But when Linden saw her ears float by on the other side of the door, her heart began pounding its door again. This stopped her from hearing any other sound, and her ears quickly shrunk back under the door and up to the sides of her head. This was the first time Linden was annoyed at her ears.

At first, the doctor could find nothing unusual about Linden or her ears. He had all sorts of noise-making instruments arranged. He banged wooden sticks together, rang a small bell, and clashed a cymbal. Linden responded to none of these. The walls were beige. There was a slight hum from the fluorescent lighting. The doctor's voice reminded her of the man's on Sunday mornings, when she listened to the sucking sounds her legs made as she pulled them up off the varnished pew.

Then a cello solo came onto the PA system in the waiting room. Linden could hear it through the door. She closed her eyes.

Linden remembered one Sunday afternoon when her family had gone for a walk on the Bruce Peninsula Trail. Her mother pronounced her identification of bird calls. Her father had a large stick that he used to tap on the ground and tree trunks. Her brother listened to his walkman.

Linden heard layers and layers and layers of sound. They swirled in her mind, a kaleidoscope, in and out like skaters at a Christmas fantasy. At that time, Linden thought that listening to a symphony was more interesting than listening to a solo. She had not wanted to listen to one bird call, or the sound of a stick, when there was the air and the water and the grass, the ground under her feet – murmuring, moaning, giggling all at once, through birds, crickets, stones.

But as Linden listened to the cello solo, she heard different interwoven feelings. There was the happy and the sad; each took the other's hands and they twirled about in tight circles. Or they pushed and shoved against each other until her muscles formed a thin hard line. She sat on the edge of her chair, her fingers gripping its edge in sweaty curve. Linden forgot the silly doctor. She forgot her mother's nervous tapping foot. The cello was inside her head. Or she was on a long slide made up of its melody and all she could do was flow along its up and down surface.

When the melody ended, Linden looked up. The doctor was staring at her. Then he began talking to her parents. Since the words had too many syllables for her to understand, Linden ignored them. Later, in the car, Linden asked her parents what had made the music in the waiting room. Her mother shrugged. Her father said he had not noticed. Linden wondered how they had not heard.

Linden's doctor consulted another doctor. Between them, they came up with a plan. They would prepare Linden's ears so that they would behave themselves. This would allow Linden to develop normal social relationships with her peers.

"Linden doesn't talk very much, does she?" they asked Linden's mother.

"No, no, she doesn't – she's a very quiet girl," replied her mother.

The doctors nodded wisely. "That is important," they said. "The more she talks, the less she will listen. Then her ears will stop growing. So we will try two things. We will teach her to talk non-stop. And we will create so many boring, non-stop noises about her that she will stop listening to anything. To anything, that is, in particular."

And that is what they did. Linden spent many hours in a room with ten tvs that talked ten different channels at once. The doctors put a walkman on her head and she was not allowed to remove it. They stood in front of her with cue cards and made her read them again and again. Since her ears were so full of all the noises around her, she could not hear own voice. But that was not the point.

And it soon worked. Linden forgot about the moon. She forgot the sun's shoes. She was learning about Barbie dolls, Mutant Ninja Turtles, and Ghostbusters. For her first day in kindergarten, she had to have her ears pierced and her first perm done. She knew all the lyrics to the latest songs and tried to keep her walkman adjusted to the same station blasting from her brother's.

Most important of all, Linden began to be afraid of silence. She forgot the different touches silence had, its colours. She forgot how it hung between some sounds as light paper chains, that it could fall suddenly like a black axe. And she forgot her favourite melody. Silence had grown between its notes like the green grass of spring. The last notes were like the small white and purple flowers that grew in their front yard, out of the melting face of winter.

And so Linden went through elementary and junior high. She learned to out-talk her parents, friends, uncles and aunts. Then came a day in grade ten. She had finished volleyball practice and was pulling her winter coat from her locker. She noticed the batteries for her walkman were dead. She walked to the main floor, passing the auditorium. Then she heard the cello.

She stopped. She felt the one line of music come at her. Invisible in the air, it divided just before her face, and swooped in two flights past her temples. The sound skidded to two halts, bumping against her ears. She felt them fumbling. So many sounds had woven about her ears, round and round and round, each tying its separate knot. There was the cello solo, in delicate fingers, untying each knot.

As the knots untied, Linden began to hear silence. She hunched her shoulders, walking quickly to the front door. For silence now wore a great white veil. It draped over the ends of sentences and goodbyes, tickled the edge of sleep. For years now, Linden had been afraid to go to bed.

But the cello solo was doing its work. The last knot slipped loose. The melody slid into her ears. She heard, for the first time, in years.

First, Linden heard the cello, its notes shadow dancing with the quiet about it. Then she began to hear each note as a prism, that cut its own tone to smaller tunes, brilliant in endless sides and angles. The melody was a tightrope, strung across the silence of space. Linden suspended herself on it on one big toe. She was not afraid of falling. She could see no end to the tightrope; she wanted it to go on and on. Indeed, the silence about her seemed to hold her up. She put her hands to her ears; with her fingertips she felt their changing shapes. Now she could touch what she was hearing.

Linden listened to the cello teacher practice in the auditorium. She asked him to teach her to play. He did not seem to mind the flowers and leopards that grew out of the sides of her head.

Within weeks, her ears began to hover just above the cello strings. One day, they took the shapes of two slender white hands. They played notes between the notes Linden played, strung Christmas lights of unknown colours about the melody. Sometimes they circled one another, two boxers, preparing to damage and be damaged. At other times, they outlined dancers, seeming to move in and out of one another – two in one, one in two, the space between, the third shape ... so many, the frail, ever changing shapes of the heart, its in-between song.

laura is like her hair

a blond constellation, northern lights
floating about the eyes,
face, an uncharted region –
that inner cosmos we tuck under memory,
and travel
foot bound through whimsical telescopes,
searching the occasional star.

laura wears the trends
and tendencies of earth,
learns its dialects
as the second language
diplomacy requires,
and often, there is the startled moment
carried by the one interrupted
in the course of another dialogue
spoken before and around
you.

there are spaces, times
we will not conquer –
that sudden, great sense of self,
the inner pocket become universe,
layered space upon space;
it will not wait
forever within time
for discovery;
many have been sucked into it
without knowing – you can see
the vortex that was eye.

laura leaves map and compass
next to the satellite tv guide.
she floats into herself.
it is home, not void,
space of nebula and planets
in her eyes a place you know
she wanders out of reach,
before genesis and the word,
beyond this earth gripped shore.

after the star

my brother plays jazz, wanders
all across the evening,
fingerprints on the darkening edge
of silence shift ...
there in the twilight
black cat on the october lawn,
its eyes two
drifting yellow places.

we are all surprised at the lives we are becoming.
the old melodies suspend themselves
in the lifting of a tea cup;
between the ticks of the clock
time spreads out in hollows –
there are landscapes,
angles of odysseys,
between 12
and 12:01.

we measure fact by faith,
syncopate and harmonize
to internal reference points,
eccentric metronomes
ambiguous only to those
who live outside our skin.
the lids of the past
hang heavy over the eyes,
half closed venetians.
memory wraps itself
around the fourth finger
like a wedding band
its smile in the mirror
is dull gold.

those on the other side of skin
do not realize aquamarine is
more than an unravelling elbow,
footsteps on the verandah
bring someone with a face
other than that in the overcoat.
at intervals, the wind opens a diary
of well thumbed thought.

light hesitates on the edge of sky.
was yesterday the green jacket
of a backyard child,
hair a full blown peony
gone blond?
we wear the layers of time
like skin,
can no longer assume
the day is merely raining,
that it is the absence of cloud
letting through the sun.

the skull cups the face
as hands, water;
between the joints of weekdays,
we touch our puny death –
it is the face in the doily,
the key ring's shadow.

on the verandah stairs,
beside the night blackened forsythia bush,
i watch the burnt out hearts
of stars travel
away from their death.
i do not know how long
a body carries the burning
light – if the loss
of our star comes before
the first light begins the distance
it must walk
between our faces.

in the unlit living room
my brother plays jazz,
all across the evening,
wanders.

reality base

valerie takes her body from the wall
and leaves her shadow pinned
there for the executioners to pinpoint
to some dark outline
with all the holes
in their excuses

she exults in her shadow –
her second hand spare
that grants her freedom as
she hastens back to her lover
who shows the underside of skin
as leaves under the agony
of wind, but he sees only her reflection
in the rounded bottom
of his tears

"but they shot my shadow"
she insists. "i am here – feel
my breasts, breath, tongue"

the robin tells her:
shadows grant dimension.
now you have the texture
of paper – you can slide through
the crack in a door,
the chasm of a heart,
the space between your lover's fingers,
his laughter

valerie goes back to the executioners.
their bullets hurt
and her shadow pours through –
dark,
blood.

genetics

we were all pre-remembered
unformed dancers restless
in dreams of those
now gone to the relief of stone;
we who flung ourselves
small wind devils
sand spectres
awaiting definition
the flesh of recognition:

ida wanders, far from the preacher
his chasm of words
their line of craggy teeth
(she fears to stand
at the cliff edge
of his black thoughts –
fears the shale will break
beneath her sole hold
on sky
and sun's breath)

she escapes the potato peels
and deformed apples
in slumber climbs
high the peaks of silence
into sky of mind
cloud unthought

syllables of wind

she watches a precipice
explored at moon fingertip
its jagged lip
in whitelit quiet.
beyond the unworded
black fall – its border
this ragged silver line
of promise

ida shakes off
the edge of awareness;
the preacher climbs into their bed
heavy with nouns, objects
he wrestles and pins to definition
for sunday's congregation . . .
even in sleep he pounds
their bed
rocks their bodies
on waves broken
to diamond tips
and thorns

sometimes awake
ida draws a jagged line
through a tabletop of flour
into garden dirt.

wants a picket fence
the preacher, in anger, denies.
"we know the straight line
we walk to God."
the words, sharp edged,
cut his mouth.
he bleeds, surprised.

the preacher's love for ida
is direct – straight line
the "i" subject
projected to object.
she is wary as verb
moves toward and away
tangential. she knows
the dark wild whispers
pull at fingers
that cling to the cliff edge
under the cock eyed moon.
she knows the voices
stab as spears.
she cannot fly.

with morning eyes she notes
her fingers, scraped raw.
she bleeds, surprised.

her daughter is born
jagged birthmark across back;
ida touches it, worries
often a grand niece
embroiders a ragged theme
into court ladies skirts.

later a half mad vancouver artist
slashes every figure's head
along an uneven brow
and finally the crazy yellow line
conceives in the dark arizona eyes
of a boy drawn, unpredictably north
to an arctic madness
the glacial edge.

the seduction of mary eve

she wears a snake with many heads
about her neck, all well spoken,
knowing the dialects of perspective,
the forked words. she says it
slithers from her first apple
out between her teeth, purring –
it is the movement of apple wine
on her tongue; it purrs like a cat,
has the half moons of a cat's false doze –
green, and wraps itself,
a reptile's caress,
about her neck.

then it has one head, speaks with an ethiopian accent
of seductions of full tongue
on virgin skin, the layers
of peach and almond,
the sugars of opium,
potassium cyanide.

the second head begins
its humid whisper about her neck
as she drapes her breasts
across the belly of silk
in a ganges riverboat; it moans
of textures of breath on skin,
the crumbling of flesh to dirt
in the hands of a lover. "the lips
of earth will be as moist," it promises,
"you will be fully pleased."

about her neck the third
joins the chant of monks
who shuffle to the night edge
of precipices sudden as hawk's scream.
"faith hears the inner voice,"
mocks the tibetan head. "bend
over the abyss and you will hear
in this cave within cave within
silences of the pebble,
the last generation of stone."

and in salem, about her neck the fourth
stretches against her cheek, whines of the scent
of burnt womb, the perfume of men's hatred,
their honeyed rhetoric, meaning's stench.
she scents the forests in her eyes, the cauldron
of her mind; suddenly in the taller shadow
of man, she feels hot embers
beneath her flesh, smells the smoke
of his glance.

mary eve thought her flesh white
but as the blood red fifth winds its head
down between her eyes, she sees
shadows of blood that snake
her undersurface. she observes reptiles
stem the flower, flower the man,
man the corporate phallus
of the skyscraper. and she sees
new york decrees liberty as woman
but she is blind and has not felt
in her stone gut, the slither
of the red snake, tasted the nightshade
on its tongue. now mary eve knows
she seduced the snake about her neck
with her longing to see beyond
her own skin.
the first lesson she will teach
this stone woman of liberty
is the taste of the apple –
the mortality of its flesh.

PERIPHERAL VISION

He rubs up against the house. Starts at the west entrance, drags around, pressing in. In the unlit kitchen, rotate with him. His hard shoulder pushes through the walls, the air. Each breath shoves a fist up the throat.

Around to the east side, along the east porch wall. On the kitchen windowsill, the large bread knife reflects a bleary moon. Small rivulets of blood lace its surface. Pick it up, run its smooth sides along skin. Listen.

He stops at the bedroom window.

"Oooooooooo, scary," Marlyss said. She leaned against the coffee machine in the staff lounge, and chewed on her empty styrofoam coffee cup. "You had a prowler last night? What'd you do? I bet Julie flipped out."

Liz nodded. She felt unfocussed, as if the events of last night were a pair of sunglasses, their reality still imposed between herself and this morning. She supposed her roommate had flipped. After the prowler left, Julie had spent the rest of the night crouched in the kitchen next to the cupboards, holding her boyfriend's baseball bat.

"How'd you know he was there? Is this, like, the first time he's been around?" Hand clutched to the throat of her psychedelic orange blouse, Marlyss's eyelids were hyperactive blue half moons.

The police had also asked her this. "Have you been aware of him before this, hanging around?"

No. "No," Liz had had to admit, to the police, to herself, and that was what caused her the greatest unease. Faulty plumbing was the only reason she had been awake at all; some problem with water pressure caused the toilet to emit a high pitch at erratic intervals until it was flushed. Pulled from sleep by its slow ascending whine, she had lain for a moment, debating the cold cat walk over linoleum, then pushed off the covers and walked in curled feet down the hall, past the kitchen, to the bathroom. She had not sensed the texture of ominous eyes, more depth to surrounding shadow. Shuffling back to bed, she had checked the lock, had thought only of the four hours' sleep until morning.

In the haze of returning sleep, a slight click had come from the east entrance, a door she and Julie had locked, then ignored behind its stack of old newspapers – their "recycling corner." Liz had turned over, telling herself it was a cat, or another of the old house's arthritic complaints. Her mother would have scoffed at this unease. Still, the silence held, extended like a pointing finger. Then came the sound she had been waiting for at the west door.

Bent to the height of the kitchen cupboards below the sink, she had crept, tension gripping her neck, back, buttocks. From the kitchen entrance, she could see the west entrance porch through one of the two glass panels that framed the door. Fortunately, the neighbors had turned on their outside lights.

Liz and Julie had often argued the need for outside lighting, but it came down to Liz's refusal to spend money on it. In Julie's opinion, it came down to Liz's mother making another posthumous grab at Liz's life. "She sits there in your face, sometimes," Julie hesitated, "like, more than memory." Julie considered herself a poet.

Crowded against the kitchen wall, Liz had peered around the corner. As far as she could see, the porch stood empty. She had relaxed, straightened. There was no one there. Just check to make sure.

She had moved up to one of the glass panels, needing a closer angle to check out the blind spot behind the door. As she had placed her hands on the glass, pressed her nose against the cold surface, a tall black form moved suddenly from the hidden space behind the door. Stooped down toward her, the face up against the glass, one hand superimposed upon hers. It had been black against her pale fingers – bigger, longer, without impression of colour or depth; the figure had loomed above and against her, black against the brown red of the porch floor, taking up most of the night between the two rusting white poles that held up a crumbling porch roof. On either side of the glass, their breath had fogged small circles.

Then he had moved, had gone, disappearing into the sound of receding footfalls. Liz had been held, pressed against the glass a moment longer, until one hand slipped, moist from the sweat of her palm. In its new spot, the glass had been startlingly cold.

She had backed into the kitchen, knocking the phone to the floor. The handset had rolled into the west entrance. She had begun to shake.

Christ, the problem's gone now, she had scolded. Don't get jumpy over a noisy phone. Mom would handle this like a lost credit card.

Still in the dark, she had dialed the police, given the officer her name, address, phone number, her reason for calling. Had been put on hold, then repeated all of the information a second time. Had been told a car was on its way. As she hung up, Julie had been coming down the stairs. "Exciting phone call?" she had yawned, switching on the lights.

It had taken ten minutes for the police to respond. Friendly, courteous, concerned, they had assured Liz they would scout the area, keep their eyes open. On their advice, Liz had turned on the three outside lights. "That bugger," she had muttered to Julie. "There goes some of my vacation money for that trip to Quebec City."

Hooking the screen door, Julie had tersely replied, "You

might not get to Quebec City if we don't spend the money on safety.

"Just pisses me off," Liz had shrugged. "I'll hook the other one."

She had left Julie in the darkened kitchen, clutching the baseball bat, and shuffled back to bed. Considering herself less susceptible to melodrama, Liz had still burrowed with unusual intensity into the sheets and blankets. After what had seemed like hours, she heard Julie go back upstairs.

In the morning, the outside lights were out, the bulbs unscrewed in their sockets.

"Holy shit!" marvelled Marlyss. She had chewed her way through half of the styrofoam cup. "Y'mean he came back, after all that? And you didn't hear him?"

"I guess not," said Liz. "Got any Tylenol? Bum me a smoke? Christ, I've got a headache. My car burst something again today."

"Get a new one, Liz – you can afford it."

"Hey – it's my alter ego, y'know? Did you say you had any Tylenol?"

The after work crowd was consoling, bought Liz several gin and tonics. She listened, settled in among the suits, tight skirts, and her headache, making sure she nodded in the correct places as Marlyss related the prowler story. After all, she was the one with pain knocking at her temples, and Marlyss was better with an audience. Much better. Liz composed a cool, detached expression for the admiring looks of the others. Then Marlyss drove her home and sat on the curb, waving her cigarette and jabbering as Liz lifted the hood to the rusting brown Impala.

"Hey Marlyss – could you turn the motor on? Don't worry about the windshield wipers – I can't get them to stop."

"Well, okay – is your heater belt still broken?"

"Not broken," Liz said reprovingly. "Just stretched . . . or something."

"It's still broken," Marlyss hollered through the open window. She clambered out of the car, twisting her heel.

"You all right? Marlyss – you're such a twit. Anyone who walks around – tries to walk around – in heels like that."

"I am a short person and I have a complex." Marlyss grinned, her active expression accentuated by the carnival colours of her make-up.

Liz returned her throbbing attention to the dark lugubrious shapes that lurked under her car hood. "I think it's this thingamajigger here that's loose. Got any recently chewed bubblegum? Krazy Glue?"

The second night, she awoke to hear voices at the west door. As she stumbled, blinking, into the brightly lit kitchen, Liz saw Julie, shoulders hunched, talking to the same two policemen of the previous night. Julie was holding the baseball bat.

"We chased him half a block with the dog," the older man was saying. "He got into one of the apartment blocks down there."

"Which one?" Julie demanded, her voice tight.

"Brown one, at the corner," the other said, breathing heavily. "He got in with a key, so we couldn't follow. By the time we could've woken someone up to let us in, he'd be safe inside whichever apartment he lives in . . . or out the back door."

"What happened?" Sleep refused to give up, shifted around in her head.

"He unscrewed the light bulbs again," said Julie. "2 a.m., this time. I saw them go out."

"We'll be in the area," the older man assured. "We patrol Strathcona, south of Whyte. It'd be a good idea to wire over those bulbs, if you get a chance. Good night."

"You sat up with the bat again, didn't you?" Liz accused, hooking the screen.

"I'm moving out, Liz," Julie said. "I can't live like this."

"What d'you mean, live like this? It's only been two nights."

"These kind of things can go on and on. And even when he decides to stop, when'll we know?"

"Okay, so he's not going to put up a sign: SORRY I GOT BORED. PLEASE DON'T TAKE IT PERSONALLY. C'mon, Julie – he's just some moral defect who's left some footprints on our property."

"Liz – Bert and I were going to get engaged soon anyways. I'll just be moving in a little earlier. I'll pay you next month's rent." Julie put a hand on Liz's shoulder. "Look – I know your mom left you this place and all, but you really should think of selling, Liz. For your own sanity. Really."

That morning, Julie began moving out, said she would spend the night at Bert's. Well, that's fine, thought Liz, rephrasing her roommate ad for the *Edmonton Journal*, if you have a boyfriend to move in with. Why wouldn't the correct words come out of her pen? She paused, looked around. Even with Julie's possessions strewn up and down the early morning stairs, the house felt different, as if it had acquired more space, allowed more room to breathe. Liz pondered. Maybe she would wait awhile with that ad.

"We should set up a prowler patrol," Marlyss yelled, competing with 630 CHED. "We could get some of the guys from work to help – could get good for your social life."

Liz glared. Over beer, frequent helpful suggestions tended to erupt from Marlyss's mouth regarding Liz's social life, or the lack thereof.

Her outline a mass of emerald green, scarlet, and mauve parrots, Marlyss squirmed. "Ah geez, Liz, can't you take a joke? I think this is kind of exciting."

"Exciting?!"

"Ah, maybe exciting isn't exactly the right word," Marlyss said hastily. "Let's go see a show – something to take your mind off this. The early show – you're tired. I'll pay."

"Marlyss, you are a dear," said Liz, brightening.

Marlyss pulled at her hair, teasing it upward. "Um, how 'bout *Fatal Attraction?*"

"Of sorts," Liz defined.

The sounds come from the west door. She creeps along, like the first time, close to the floor. Julie's bat is on the counter, lit faintly by the neighbor's outside light. Slowly, she peers into the west entrance.

No shape on the west porch. The lights are out again. She straightens, moves to look through the glass panel for the blind spot behind the door. As she leans her face against the glass, remembers its coldness, the tall black form looms up against her, hands pressed to the glass – black hands, long fingers stretched out in gloves. Large. They press, closer. Closer. They are coming through the glass. Not breaking it. His hands are through and the beginning of the wrists. His arms. She screams now, backing away. Screams.

Awake. She was awake. Liz sat up, looked wildly for the alarm clock. 12:30. She had set it for 1 a.m. Suddenly, she was afraid of her bedroom doorway – afraid to look at its black empty space, afraid not to look. She sat, locked into position ten minutes before she was able to shift a hand, move her face towards the door, place her feet on the floor.

Shuffling into the kitchen, she rehearsed. Screen doors are hooked and inside doors locked. Outside lights are on. He'd have to smash windows to get in and doesn't want to make that much noise – neighbours haven't left on their sabbatical yet. Liz ran her fingers across the glass panels at the west entrance. Their surfaces were smooth, unperturbed. Only a dream.

Calmer now, she yawned, shaking her head. Fatigue pressed against her temples and face like two hands. What did Mom do, those nights she couldn't sleep? Towards the end, it had been almost every night. In the dark kitchen, Liz plugged in the kettle, groped in the cupboards to find the

Nescafé. Smaller than the honey, stupid. Mom must've read this house like Braille. She never woke you up.

The cupboards and counter felt colder in the dark. Liz noticed the rough edges on cupboards where the canary yellow paint had chipped off. Sky blue underneath, she reminded herself, from before we repainted.

Died two years ago, and she's still here sometimes, Liz thought – moving around, running her finger along a windowsill, murmuring over a house plant. There had been no one to notify, when the illness had progressed to the point of hospitalization – no grandparents, siblings, long lost cousins. Mom had hated her family, cut them off, said they destroyed everyone they touched and they would not get at her daughter. Well, they had gotten Mom in the end, through her genes.

Congenital disease, Liz thought, sitting inside, waiting. There was a loud bang. Ouch! Shit! She had walked into the garbage pail and barked her shin. On the other side of the kitchen, the kettle wheezed. As she reached for the plug, she passed her hand through the steam. Shit! He hasn't even shown up and here I am, doing his job for him. She sucked her hand and rubbed her leg. The west porch light went out.

The cops. The cops. Her hand went for the phone, then paused, wavered mid air over the handset. Why?

She would give her name, address, phone number, probably two, three times.

The east porch light went out.

They would show up, courteous, friendly, concerned, probably having chased him half a block. Their description would match hers – no name, no face. Tall, lean, dressed in black. Big deal.

Tentative, she moved from the phone, checked through her bedroom doorway. The back light was out. Christ, you should've wired the bulbs instead of going to the goddam movie with Marlyss. The back yard stared through her window, implacable. Even with the inside lights out, she could not see much. Where was the bastard? She peered through the window, squinting.

A living room floorboard creaked on the west side. Her heart jerked her body forward with each pound. C'mon Liz, handle it. There was no outside noise. Under the grey skyline, the bare black arms of April trees held motionless. Further up 108 Street, she could see the brown of a trunk lit up by street lights.

Suddenly, her eyes darted sideways, caught by a small red glow which appeared around the west corner. It moved mid air, with a slight up and down movement, along the west fence to the back of the yard, then slowed, moved downward, and stopped. Her eyes widened. She watched as the ember glowed brighter, then dulled. Fuck the bugger. He was so casual, she felt a smile hesitate on her mouth. Smoking in my back yard, in my patio swing, on my goddam time. Fuck you.

She was angry, strode to the kitchen, phoned the police. She gave her name, address, phone number three times, waited, pacing the house in tight, territorial circles. The police were quick to respond, but the small red glow had disappeared by the time she had gotten off the phone.

"You haven't wired your bulbs," pointed out the older cop. "You really need to light up this area."

"I'll do it tomorrow," Liz promised impatiently. "He sat there and smoked. Couldn't you take the butt as evidence or something?"

"It might be a little difficult to find right now," said the older dubiously.

"We'll screw in the back bulb and look," the younger decided. Liz had the uncomfortable feeling he was humouring her.

He had not left the butt. Liz fell asleep about 5:30, shoved herself into awareness at seven by rolling onto the cold linoleum and lying there spread eagled. Tylenol sketched its superficial netting over the headache.

As the elevator hummed its way to the office floor, Liz avoided her four reflections in the walls of mirrors. They pressed in on her, their copycat gestures too close. Must be the headache, she thought, escaping, then spotted the blond teased hair, the tongue caught between teeth.

"Marlyss – come help me with my car," Liz said, passing a hand between her friend's pink eyelids and pink tipped typing hands.

Startled, Marlyss looked up from her desk, removed her headphones, eyes wide beneath their vivid eye shadow. "God, Liz – you look like you drew those circles under your eyes with eye liner. Did he show up again? Is that why you're late?"

"Yes," said Liz tersely. "And so did the demon who inhabits my car. I need your help – before it starts raining."

"Okay." Marlyss gave a satin sky blue shrug and followed Liz down the stairwell, not questioning her avoidance of the elevator. "Oh my god!"

Liz put her arm around Marlyss's padded shoulders letting her weight sag against her friend. "I do believe I have found the original Chev Impala – the model they chucked in favor of the one that worked. That one they put on the assembly line. This one they sold to me."

Bent along a crease, the hood reared in the middle, so that it stood in an upside down V fold above the motor. "I dunno, Marl – I just tried to open it this morning, to see if I could fix the windshield wipers. What do I do? What do I do with this piece of Chevy shit?"

"We'll have to flatten it." Marlyss climbed onto the back trunk in her heels, her odd crawling movements tightened by her skirt. Somewhere on the car roof, her nylons announced a tear. Liz was laughing so hard it had become difficult to breathe. With one high heeled foot, Marlyss shoved delicately at the peak of the hood, trying to push it forward. In a rusty protest, the hood began to move. Slowly, she was able to crawl onto it, wobbled briefly in a standing position, then jumped gently to flatten it. "This what you wanted?"

Arms flung grandly out, Marlyss's gesture outlined her bra clearly through the flimsy material of her blouse. Her skirt had inched up one one hip, and her streaked blond hair was anything but demure. Laughter drained the tension Liz had carried to work. Suddenly she loved the uncomplicated, one dimensional methods Marlyss used to cope. "Yes. Yes. This is exactly what I wanted. Thank you, Marlyss. Thank you."

Marlyss crawled off the hood with a delighted smile. "Anything to please," she giggled. "You know me."

That night, it rained. Liz spent the hours reading and pruning her plants by flashlight in the kitchen, huddled next to the cupboards on the floor. Every now and then, she moved around the house, peering out of the windows. The neighbour's house stood empty. Must've left for their sabbatical, she thought. There was no sign of him.

It was more than the lack of sound that told her this, more than the unperturbed black curtain outside her window, unpenetrated by the butt end of his breath. When he was out there, the air pushed invisible shoulders against her, refused to give her room, as if space gained an additional dimension. Tonight, the house was her own, unthreatened.

"It's yours and mine, Mom," Liz said softly, playing with the ivy. "Our Fortress." The night curled around her like the sound of her mother's breathing, remembered from times Liz had pretended to fall asleep on her mother's shoulder in the middle of a book being read aloud to her. She felt the regular rise and fall of that memory now in her own breathing; it expanded her own sense of lung space, pushed back the outside places.

Breathing rhythm had been the most frightening part of her mother's deterioration, breaths sounding like hands that were losing grip on a cliff edge. Liz shook herself out of the memory, went to bed at 3 a.m., slept until her 7 a.m. alarm. Even with the extra hours of sleep, it was hell to get up.

That morning, Marlyss chattered hyperspeed, grated like a temporary solution used once too often. Stop thinking that, Liz scolded herself. Yesterday, she was a godsend.

"D'you have any Tylenol, Marl?"

"You need help getting to your desk?" said Marlyss, giggling. "He show up again last night?"

"No," Liz mumbled. "Probably because of the rain."

"Pardon?" demanded Marlyss.

"You're yelling," moaned Liz.

"No I'm not," said Marlyss. "I can hardly hear you. Hey – there's a new supervisor down the hall – see over there? He's the one in the dark suit looking at us."

Liz noticed the tall, slightly balding man at the front desk observing them. As Marlyss, in practiced confusion, dropped her gaze gracefully to the floor, Liz glared back. Balding male, she thought. This does nothing for my headache. "See you at lunch, Marlyss," she muttered and groped her way to her desk.

Four Tylenol later, the supervisor introduced himself. "Larry Spuderman," he said, extending his hand.

"Liz Erickson." She tried to smile, holding two fingers in what she hoped was an obvious gesture, against her left temple. His checkered suit seemed to be imprinting itself against her brain.

"You don't look well."

"I haven't been sleeping very well."

"I heard – from Marlyss," he said. "A prowler."

Fuck her.

"I hear you need some help wiring your outside bulbs. I'm pretty tall. I'd be glad to help out." He pushed some papers aside and sat down on the edge of her desk. Liz pointedly picked them up and moved them to the other side of her typewriter, but he appeared oblivious. "Really, it's no problem." He leaned forward and smiled. "Marlyss said she'd hold the chair for me. Y'know – hold it steady while I work the pliers."

A real social event. "Sure, it'd be a real help."

It took them several hours, most of her gin, and more of her Tylenol before Larry clipped the last wire. By this time, Marlyss was a crumpled yellow heap on the sofa, singing softly to herself. She managed a faint cheer as Liz turned on the three lights. From the chair, Larry grinned down at Liz, handing her the pliers. His eyes began to unravel her sweater.

"Shall we go out and celebrate?"

"I'm sorry. I think I need to catch some z's," she said firmly, "Thanks for your help, though." Her tone caught up with him and rapidly reknit the sweater's bodice. "Perhaps Marlyss?"

On the sofa, there was evidence of an attempt to focus. Marlyss sat up.

"On second thought," Larry sighed, "I do have some work to do for tomorrow."

Body slightly incoherent from the effects of the gin, Marlyss straggled out the door disconsolately. "Dallas is on tonight," Liz told her comfortingly. "Want me to call a cab?"

At midnight, she awoke, found four hours' sleep had not erased the headache. Tylenol bottle in hand, Liz plugged in the kettle. The outside lights were on, fortified with one hundred watt bulbs. With their help, she should be able to point this guy out in a crowd by his shadow.

En route to the coffee, her hand slid into a lump of butter. Jesus, she thought, wiping off her hand on a tea towel. How did Mom handle those all nighters without waking me up?

Too much sugar in the coffee. As she sipped the hot sweet liquid, she fingered the sugar bowl's smooth shape. From Mom's dinner set. My single Mom. Hard to do, especially in the sixties . . . and the seventies. Probably still is. This house is full of her. Too bad you can't see it in the dark – yellow cupboards, bright flowered wallpaper. What a fighter, too – leaving all this colour in her wake. Mom.

Liz frowned, rubbed at her temples, willing the throbbing to recede. The closer death came, the brighter the colours Mom had surrounded herself with, as if she fought fate in her eyes, not throughout her entire nervous system. Still, death came, its face as expected – black.

In the dark, Liz imagined some residue of her mother's spirit, some invisible outline, settle over her, into her flesh. Fortress. Liz smiled, remembering. Mom had called this house their Fortress. Fortress.

Shins alert for the garbage can, Liz shuffled into the kitchen, munching a package of barbecue chips. The headache had been absorbed into somewhere, had faded out of thought. She sighed.

The window next to the east porch was dark. Her eyes swallowed her face. There had been no sound. A click came from the west porch. As she turned, the west entrance went dark. A moment later, there was a large crash out back. Total darkness.

The air pressed in on her, refused to let her breathe. Lungs stretching, she pushed against it, stumbled to her bedroom. Out in the yard, the end of a cigarette brightened for a long instant, flickered as it was tapped. She stood in the dark, watching as it finished, slowly, luxuriously, saw it drop to the ground and go out, leaving only darkness below the grey skyline.

She knew when he left – something in the way the trees drew back from the house, stopped scratching up against the east wall. She slept.

"He clipped the wires?" Marlyss demanded, disbelieving. Liz nodded hazily, wondering how Marlyss had managed to conquer quarter tones in what was, for most, a mere speaking voice. "What about the one out back?"

"Threw a brick at it. Tore the whole thing out of the wall. He left this in the mail box." Gingerly, Liz pulled a brown paper bag out of her purse.

"A pair of wire cutters?"

"Yeah."

"You're going to take them to the police."

"I suppose so," Liz muttered. "How was Dallas?"

"Ah, the hockey game was on. Geez, Liz, they're going to have to catch this guy. You look terrible. Hey – any answer on your ad for a roommate? I think this guy Larry's interested in you. You gotta stop wearing that magenta. It's not your colour."

"It's my favorite sweater," said Liz coldly.

"Y'know, Liz, I think you should move. And the Salvation Army is next to the police station. For the sweater. Think about it."

On the weekend, Liz slept. 5:30 p.m., Friday, she closed the house curtains, opened them again Monday morning. Her bedroom window was the only exception; these drapes she pulled open, heavy as eyelids, each midnight, then sifted through the darkness, watching for the small red glow in the yard's west corner. She surrendered the outside lighting – it would become an expensive war to lose.

Tense, her body muttered with the desire to go out and shove and shove and shove him out of her yard. The need would grow, her muscles harden to contain it. He did not seem to do much besides sit on the swing and smoke, luxuriate in the amount of her time he could suck in with each drag. Bastard, she thought. Here I am, sleeping through one of the hottest May weekends in Edmonton's recorded history, and he's probably out there tanning by moonlight.

Sunday, just inside her bedroom window, she lit up a Du Maurier. It was the first light she had allowed herself in the house while he was present. She noted the way his cigarette froze mid air. Must've arrested the swing's movements with his feet, she assessed, inhaling slowly. There now, I've surprised you. Y'see – you don't control everything, you son of a bitch fuckhead.

Out on the swing, the cigarette slowly resumed its rhythm. Liz watched it carefully, tried to match its movements. Inhaled with him, exhaled, and waited. Neanderthal man discovered fire and farming between each drag. What – was he reviewing his entire family tree each time?

Keep a grip, Liz. Probably just planning the details of your rape and murder.

A few nights later, she tried moving out of his rhythm to see if he would follow. She created slight discrepancies – slightly slower, a little faster. Tilt the wrist at a different angle. Closer to the face.

She moved her cigarette end along her profile, lighting small sections of her face. No go. There was no change in his rhythm. He did not light up his profile for her. Only the small red ember at the back of her garden, night after night.

She began to wear sunglasses to work regularly to hide the dark circles around her eyes. As she adjusted to the 9 to 5 work, 6 to midnight sleep, midnight to 4 or 5 prowler watch, and the 5 to 7 sleep routine, daylight began to hurt her eyes. When she was awake in the house, Liz left the lights off. It became most familiar in the dark, receptive to her fingertips. Curtains were pulled open at night to watch, then closed for daylight.

Her four plants were beginning to brown, gain sharp edges. She named them Chocolate Bunny, M and Ms, The Sahara at High Noon, and at the end of a headache, The Defecation.

Marlyss had left her another threatening note, written in bright red ink: MEET ME FOR A DRINK AFTER WORK IF YOU VALUE OUR FRIENDSHIP! The conditional tense, Liz mused, wondering if Marlyss understood its meaning. Ah, she'd go tonight. Her body had begun to adjust to its new schedule and could afford the loss of a few hours' sleep. It was enough stress at work trying to avoid Larry Spuderman without adding Marlyss to the list. THE TWISTED ONION OKAY? she wrote back.

The after work crowd was bathed in the usual purple neon. Liz removed her sunglasses, slipped in between an accountant and an articling lawyer, and ordered a gin and tonic.

"Larry and I are seeing each other," Marlyss yelled at her, her face and hair varying shades of purple.

Liz grimaced inwardly. "And how d'you feel about that?" she hollered back.

"Oh, great!" Marlyss hooted, clutching her beer bottle with long dark purple nails. "It doesn't bother you, does it?"

"Why would it?" Irritation lacerated her words. Jesus – and this was her friend?

"Well, I realize you sort of had this thing for him when he first started work," Marlyss smirked. "Larry and I hope this won't interfere with our friendship."

Liz pondered the cocktail list. "Don't worry, Marlyss – I got over it . . . pretty damn quick."

The purple hair ducked down for a drink, and Liz glanced away, knowing her scorn had been too obvious. About to look back at her friend, apologize, she caught the eyes of a man seated a few tables away. Watched – I'm being watched.

The back of her throat tightened, she started to look away, then caught herself. Why should I? To accommodate? To accommodate what? Fear hunched where she wanted to swallow. He was not moving his eyes from her face. Looking away makes it his territory. God damn it, it's my face.

She cradled her chin on her hands, resisting the urge to pull her eyes away, move her chair so that her shoulder and back protected her face from his eyes. How long has it been since the last sex? Year? Year and a half?

Some sudden decision pulled her body up, walked her

over to his table. She could taste the anger in her mouth, feel the tension, desire, outlining her like an invisible skin. She asked him to dance, did not resist as he pulled her in close, fingering the short hairs on the back of her neck. Warm – he was warm, solid. The body under the purple flannel shirt gave slightly under her fingers. The flicker of heart at his purple throat made him real.

Jim. His lips said he was Jim … Jim an electrician, albeit a purple electrician, with an address and a phone number – she made sure of that. And he did not smoke.

When he made a move, later, to turn off his bedside lamp, she protested, saying she wanted to see him as they made love, wanted to see the colour of his eyes, the different browns that ran through his hair. She watched all of his movements, kissed with her eyes open, ran her fingers over the places the coral in his skin darkened to its beginner tan. As they lay quietly, listening to their breathing lengthen, she became aware of the night sky beyond the half open curtains. Unease shifted like a submerged swimmer. There was the sudden image of a cigarette glowing at the back of her yard – approaching, approaching the house.

Their house. Fortress.

"What time is it?"

Jim looked puzzled. "'Bout ten. What is it, Sarah?"

Liz began to dress. Sarah. It was the first name that had come to mind. She had never lied about her name before. She had felt the need, suddenly, at the Twisted Onion. Now, it felt unnecessary. "I think I'd better go."

"I'm sorry. I enjoyed that, thought maybe you could stay the night."

Uncomplicated, one dimensional, she thought, flushing. "I'd like to. I'm sorry – I have something I have to take care of."

He shrugged. "Let me give you my number. Call me sometime?"

10:30, she thought, keeping the last kiss hovering on her mouth as she drove the Chev home. If I set the alarm for two, I can get in four, maybe five hours of sleep tonight. That'll have to do until tomorrow.

As she parked the car on 85th Avenue, she noticed the west screen door swinging in the breeze. She ran up to catch it; the flimsy wood swung with unusual vehemence against the wall of the house. The inside door stood open.

Fear opened wide in her throat. The house sat, full of darkness; she could hear nothing moving. In front or behind – where was he? A void opened at her back. The night was not one shadow, it was made of thousands, shifting, interweaving. Liz turned, twisted her ankle slightly on the step, ignoring the wedge of pain as she backed up against the house. It began to rain.

She moved away from the doorway, along the wall, off the end of the porch. Drops of water slapped against her face, and she continued, back to wall, away from the porch, watching the doorway. The door swung open slowly, then slammed into the wall. She broke into a run, stumbled against the Chev.

Can't get the key into the lock. The hot salt mix of tears and mascara was blinding. No one in the back seat.

"MOTHER OF TWO YOUNG CHILDREN MURDERED." In the subway. Today's headlines.

The nearest police station was downtown, so she drove to a pay phone and called, then paced out the few minutes until the cruiser arrived. Different officers this time – courteous, friendly, concerned.

"Prowler?"

She nodded. "The door's open. I was afraid to go in alone. I didn't know what'd be inside."

"We'll come check it out with you," the older one said. "Would you stay in your car, miss?"

As she parked in front of the house, she saw the screen

door still swinging in the wind. The house quivered and crumpled with each pound of her heart. In spite of their demands they go alone, she followed the officers up the sidewalk. It was nothing like the movies – they did not clutch corners, slink after their shadows, though they were careful, following their flashlight beams, turning on lights as they went.

The house was empty, seemed undisturbed. She could see nothing out of place, could not feel any other presence. The two men looked at her questioningly. Unwilling to let them leave, she hesitated.

"D'you thing you could've left it open this morning?"

"No." Now she was uncertain. "I'm pretty careful. Well, maybe . . . I dunno."

"We'll be in the area," they assured her, and left.

She latched the screen door and locked the inside ones, then leaned up against the kitchen cupboards, staring down at the counter. Her eyes were tired, felt oversized, as if they reached back through her entire head. Two envelopes and a pizza pamphlet lay next to her hand, blurring gently into the counter linoleum. Two envelopes. She picked them up slowly – a letter from a school friend and a bank statement. Today's mail. He must have brought it in.

She began to shake, dropping the mail on the counter. He had gotten in. How? She knew she had locked the door. Knew it. And why today? Had there been other times? How often had he been inside this house?

He isn't here now – inside. He's not here now, Liz. The screen doors are hooked. He can't get in now. Not now. Stop it. Stop shaking. Stop.

He was not on the patio swing that night. When she went to look, still sleepless at 2 a.m., it took her a short time to locate him. Finally, she found his shape, crouched on the back shed roof, ten feet from her bedroom window. She sucked in her breath, felt it cold in her mouth, her stomach. As she watched, the red ember glowed brightly, then dulled.

It began in her gut, mounted her throat. In a sudden movement, she unlatched the one section of her bedroom window that opened. Low pitched, the words came out, hissed through the night air, hysteria in her voice. The form did not move.

"You bastard. Get off my property. Get away from my house. This is my house. My home. Fortress."

The cigarette end flickered. Then she heard the rain begin, its cool sweet drops, the gurgling of the clogged drainage pipe in the basement. Laughed – she threw back her head, felt laughter take her lank body. The drumming outside increased.

The shape on the roof faded. The rain washed him away, like any other dirt.

Dizzy, empty headed, giggles still clawing at her abdomen, Liz opened the west door, stumbled down the porch to the back yard. As the rain poured down, she swung around in a circle, mouth open, sucking in wetness. She sat on the back yard swing and rocked, then ran inside, fetched her cigarettes and smoked one on the swing. With the help of a kitchen chair, she climbed the shed and straddled its peak, thumping her chest to resonate her Tarzan yell. Then, wet hair and clothing clinging to her like another sense, she went inside.

Her body had released so much tension, its relaxed state gave her more pleasure than the sex, a few hours previous. When she slid between the sheets, the material stroked her, slid over and around her skin. Gently, she brought herself to climax, crying out, then fell asleep to the sound of the rain.

For the next few days, it rained. Liz watched the colour come back to her face. Her skin felt smoother, less clammy. After a dead bolt had been placed on both doors, she and Marlyss secure, cradled within the sound of the rain, finished some old vodka while Liz took apart the kitchen drain. She spent another night at Jim's. Each cloudy morning created a day she could call her own, a day she owned. Then Friday dawned, clear

When she called to cancel a date with Jim, she told him she had come down with some sort of flu – the "Mozzarella Tahiti Flu." It sounded impressive enough. "Feels kind of like melted cheese," she told him, and laughing, he said he understood. His, "Call me soon, Sarah," brought a thick shame to her face, and she stood with her hand on the phone a short while after she had said goodbye. Jim was not the prowler – she knew that. Why this need to pick and choose times and places, names and faces, with him?

That night, on the shed roof, the prowler began to read to her. She had opened the bedroom window, wanting to hear his movements. From somewhere within the black shape of his body outlined against the grey of the sky, she saw him pull out a small white focus of light. There was some scraping against shingles as he settled his weight, the sound of a throat clearing itself. Then he began to read.

She was holding Julie's bat, balancing her weight against it. Smooth and curved, his voice seemed to make a gentle circular movement against her skin. The bat, too, massaged its rounded end against her hand; she brought it up against her chest and rubbed her chin against it. She had to move closer to the window, lean against the glass to catch the words.

"My beloved put her hand to the latch, and my heart was thrilled within me. I arose to open to my beloved, and my hands dripped with myrrh, my fingers with liquid myrrh, upon the handles of the bolt, I opened to my beloved, but my beloved had turned and gone. My soul failed me when she spoke. I sought her but found her not; I called her, but she gave no answer. The watchmen found me, as they went about in the city they beat me, they wounded me, they took away my mantle, those watchmen of the walls. I adjure you, O daughters of Jerusalem, if you find my beloved, that you tell her I am sick with love."

As he continued in the same sing song rhythm, Liz realized the literature was familiar but could not place it. His reading continued, gentle, erotic, then paused. In the silence, she heard him flip the pages, had time to feel oddly amused. With a full moon, this could be considered quite romantic. Then she jabbed the bat fiercely against her chin. Romantic! Fuck the screwball!

"Fuck off." She spoke in low, level tones, projected through the window. There was no response, only silence from the rooftop. She bit her lip, bouncing her chin on the bat. He continued.

"For everything there is a season, and a time for every matter under heaven: a time to be born, and a time to die; a time to plant, and a time to pluck up what is planted; a time to kill, and a time to heal; a time to break down, and a time to build up; a time to weep, and a time to laugh; a time to mourn, and a time to dance; a time to cast away stones, and a time to gather stones together; a time to embrace and a time to refrain; a time to seek, and a time to lose; a time to keep and a time to cast away; a time to rend and a time to sew; a time to keep silence and a time to speak; a time to love and a time to hate; a time for war and a time for peace; a time to rule and a time to wait."

She watched him pocket the book and flashlight, smoke another cigarette. Then he left. In the morning, she found a bible in her mailbox, marked at Ecclesiastes, Chapter Three. She noted the difference in the text. Verse eight ended with ". . . a time for war, and a time for peace." There was nothing about "rule," nothing about "wait."

Liz took the bible down to the police station. The officer looked dubious but checked it for fingerprints. There were none but her own on the cover.

"I know, I know," she said. "You can't arrest a guy for being religious."

"Isn't it nice to know he's so conservative?" Marlyss giggled. "Maybe he's trying to convert you."

"He's got a beautiful voice," Liz said. "Kind of hypnotic. After a while, you sort of slip into it."

But Marlyss was not listening. "I think Larry and I are going to move in together. You seen that guy from the bar lately?"

"Lady, I dunno why you keep this thing," the mechanic shrugged. "Your hood's the wrong geometric shape, your glove compartment doesn't close, your heater fan's missing a bearing. As a matter of fact, your whole car's missing its bearing. You got no volume control on your radio and the windshield wipers turn on automatically when you turn on the ignition. You need a new carburetor and your muffler's about to blow. I'll buy the thing off you for fifty bucks."

"That's the price of a bus pass," Liz said indignantly.

"You want me to fix all this?"

"How much?"

"Over fifteen hundred."

"D'you have a Do It Yourself Manual?"

"A Chevy Impala Impala-Yourself-A?" He laughed.

Liz's lips tightened. "D'you have it or not?"

He grinned. "Not."

"Then goodbye." Liz got into her car and slammed the door. The glove compartment door fell off. "Oh fuck it," she muttered. Fuck it, fuck it, fuck it.

After another night of rain, the prowler had passed several nights, smoking silently on the swing. Last night, he sat on the shed roof and watched. In the morning, she found two roses, their thorns removed, in her mailbox. She took them out to the patio and ground them under her heel.

Tonight, his voice was gentle. She pushed the desk back from her bedroom window and sat in an armchair, the bat between her legs, listening.

"Erik would watch the way she twisted an earring as she listened, how she had arranged a scarf about her neck, the colour of her lipstick. These were clues, indicators she unwittingly gave, pieces of a jigsaw. When he found the last clue, he would assemble the whole picture and he would have her, suddenly three dimensional, smooth as an Inuit sculpture between his hands, the way she lay in his thoughts."

"Would you fuck off?" she said loudly through the window. There was no break in his tone, although she thought it became slightly reproving.

"Mouth on her throat, he felt her pulse quicken, heard the flutter in her breath. She moaned, legs parting about him, and his hands moved up to circle her throat, seeking the pause, the question between each heartbeat. Intent upon the curve of her closed eyelids, her slightly open mouth, he carried her to the bed which lay in the room's shadow, beyond the faint light of the moon."

Alive – the surface of her skin was coming alive; a heat grew between her legs. In sharp points, sweat prickled her forehead, her breasts. Against her palms, the bat warmed, seemed to soften. Abruptly, she stood and slammed the window. Angrily lit a cigarette, dragging fiercely. Breath came in short stabs. The second cigarette crushed as she pulled it from the pack.

"You are in a rage, Liz." Her voice rasped in her ears, unbearable. How implacable he looked, smoking on that rooftop, so in control. With deliberate slowness, she settled back in the armchair and smoked, feet up against the sill, the bat on the floor and the window closed.

Dr. Theodore sat on the other side of the desk, scratching his pen across her medical file. Or across my temples, Liz thought blearily, refocussing on the doctor's hunched form between blinks. It was her semi-annual check-up.

"Problems with memory loss?" He looked up. His white skin seemed to blend into his white lab jacket.

"I can't remember," Liz joked feebly.

Dr. Theodore was a model of professional face presentation. "It's in the family, Liz. You need to keep an eye out for symptoms." The doctor was an old friend of her mother's. Liz shifted, then nodded.

"Memory loss noted?"

"No."

"Insomnia?"

Hesitation. How to answer? "Not really."

"Could you clarify?"

"Well, it's for . . . other reasons."

Across the desk, the pale eyebrows lifted. "Such as?"

"Um ... relationship problems."

Eyebrows resumed a relaxed position. "Boyfriend issues, eh?"

"You could say that."

"I miss Sarah. No one had your mother's sense of humour, Liz."

They sat a moment, draped in memory.

"Yeah," Liz muttered. "I miss her too."

A week passed before she opened the window again. It was the end of May and Edmonton was experiencing a drought. Marlyss was already deeply tanned. Colours around Liz seemed to be changing, fading. This year, spring was brown at the edges. People's faces blurred into giant fingerprints, their odd mouths distorting into syllables.

She had not phoned Jim for nine days. She picked up the phone, tried to remember his number. Tired – she was too tired. We've been out, oh, how many times? Made love ten, eleven times? What does his face look like? Brown hair. Dark? Light? Dark blue. No – the dark purple neon of the Twisted Onion

She shook her head. Blue eyes. She remembered telling him his eyes were blue with some sort of purple shot through them. Tired. Mom must've felt this way. She put the phone down.

Lips against coffee mug rim, she felt the edgy alertness that began around midnight, the only time she did not long for sleep. At five a.m., it was difficult to fall asleep, and this lasted until she got to work. Then the printed page became a hyperactive blur.

She had not decided to open the window ahead of time, thought suddenly she wanted to relieve the heat. Then she heard his voice again, felt her body lines curve gently towards it. She shook her head. I've got to phone Jim.

The voice went on and on. At first she stood, leaning against the window frame, pushing her face against the cool glass. Press, make it hurt. Keep some distance. God, he's smooth – the bugger. Gradually the chair drew her in, cradled her relaxing body. Her legs slid apart.

"In the bed's shadow, her eyes darkened, looking inward. She became a series of interiors, places for him to touch and enter, and he was hands, mouths that met her everywhere, his teeth a light insinuation on her skin. She wanted more of him, greater pressure of teeth, hands, penis. Between her legs she was widening, pleasure moving her outward. His hoarse voice traced her like fingers, causing her to raise her arms above her head, turning her first one way then another. Gradually, she was being separated by his hands, divided to a place wider than she had thought possible. He separated her, entered her slowly, inevitably, and waited."

When Liz touched herself with the bat, she came, moaning slightly in pleasure. There was silence, and as the orgasm subsided, she realized that he had heard her, was listening. Her cheeks burned.

"You didn't call me all week – I was beginning to get worried," Jim said. He leaned back on one elbow, tracing her nose, mouth, chin. "It's getting hard to concentrate on my job, Sarah."

"Am I that all encompassing?" she teased, seeking a tangent, a way out of the conversation looming ahead. She watched his mouth – its movements, textures.

"I'd like to be able to talk to you more often. I'd like to be able to call you, Sarah. How 'bout you give me your number?"

Fear curled like baby's toes in her stomach. Taking his hand from her face, she held it loosely, played with the thumb.

"Ah, Jim – y'know it's just me. I don't feel comfortable with it. I really like you. I really do. I just need the space."

"But Sarah," he said, voice gentle. She winced away from it, trying not to move physically. His hurt seeped through his fingers to her. "What about me? I don't feel comfortable with this. You matter to me now, and I can't call you. You won't tell me where you work, where you live."

She remained silent, looking down at the pillow. Silence was the safe place to crawl into. Toward and against one another, the skins of their palms curved.

"The time between your calls gets longer and longer."

Behind her eyes, tears shoved around. She tried to stop them but they insisted a presence, hot, salty. He was pulling her towards him, sliding a leg between hers, pressing her face in between his neck and shoulder. I'm not trying to manipulate, she thought fiercely. Let him fool himself, if he wants to. God, I'm so tired. Tired.

"I just can't, Jim. I can't explain. I don't have another lover. There's no one else."

His heart pulsed against her mouth. "That's not the point," he said.

Ashamed, she disentangled, pulling away. "I need to go."

"Stay the night," he said hoarsely. "Stay just one night with me. Please."

Throat, shoulders, the back of her head stiffened, began to shake. "Don't beg me, Jim. Leave it alone. You can find someone else easily enough if you need to." She was pulling on clothes, heard something rip. To one side – she was trying to keep him to one side, to the corner of her eye. He lay, pale, limp, staring at the ceiling. There was silence as she left the bedroom, closed the apartment door, though she paused in the entrance, waiting for a voice.

The Darkening Eye by Emily Gladview: it was in the mailbox. Liz flipped through it, recognizing sections. She thought of ripping it into single words and leaving it strewn about the back yard. The option held dramatic possibilities, but some cat would probably use it for kitty litter. Shrugging, grinning slightly, she left it on the counter, next to the phone.

"... as pertaining to clause 2 c, wherein neither sub-clause a nor sub-clause b of this clause 2 is deleted by the parties entering into this agreement ..." Larry's voice droned on in her headphones and she typed, "... if all of the blanks in either, but not both, submerged into ..."

She pressed stop and rewind. Not "submerged." "...but not both, of sub-clauses a or b of this clause 2 are filled in by the ... filled in by the bodies entering into this agreement ... entering into the ... agreement, into one another, into the ..."

She shook her head.

"They enter, whisper of the agreement. Whisper to one another, whisper to raise her arms, to turn. He separates her with his hands, separates her with two hands as he enters her. Whispers as he enters a place wider than she thinks possible. He enters and waits. The agreement to wait. To enter and wait."

The voice whispered through her hands, her arms. Her whole body throbbed with its rhythm. It focussed down, became an ache between her legs. When she shifted her weight forward, her panties tightened against her crotch and rubbed.

"Coming for coffee?" Marlyss had lifted the earphones off her ears.

"Pardon?" Flesh toned images shifted, then faded into Marlyss's blue make-up and coral blouse.

"Coffee, Liz. C O F F E E. Remember – black with two teaspoons sugar? It's ten o'clock – time for your break."

Her head cleared. Back to one dimension. "Oh, yeah.

Daydreaming." A sidelong glance at the page she had been typing brought the images back. Quickly, she pulled her work out of the machine. "Let's go." Her voice sounded edgy, loud, as she slipped the page into her purse. Where the hell was the incinerator?

Screaming, she awoke from the dream. Images: face down in the grass. Jim's hands, separating her, voice shifting her pelvis. His erect penis becoming longer, harder. It shoves slowly through her, to her stomach, her chest. Through to her mouth. A black shape watches from the shed roof, smoking. Whispers to Jim. Rules.

Her orgasm came as she woke, shaking her with its violence. Through the dark, she stumbled to the bathroom, turned the shower on. Held the tap to the coldest temperature.

One eyelid dragged the other down. Overtime's a killer. Liz dropped two ice cubes down the front of the t-shirt and cupped them against her breasts. Stay awake Liz, stay awake. Geez, I wish I had the guts to get a gun and shoot him.

She heard the match strike, saw the flare and the ember glow. He was sitting at the base of the shed, in its darkest shadow.

"I left your goddam bloody ring in the mailbox," she called out the window. "An engagement ring – who'm I supposed to become? Mrs. Jack the Ripper? Mrs. Boston Strangler? They weren't heroes, y'know – only assholes who needed courses on better time management. You want a hobby? How 'bout Chinese cooking? Golf? Good daylight activities. Look – I'll meet you for a coffee downtown. A real date – on well lit streets, of course. Get out of my life you fucker."

She paused. Silence. Then the small flashlight trained itself on another book. He began. "At the day and time appointed for solemnization of matrimony, the persons to be married shall come into the body of the church, or shall be ready in some proper house, with their friends and neighbours; and there standing together, the man on the right hand, and the woman on the left, the minister shall say, Dearly beloved, we are gathered together here in the sight of God and in the face of this company to join together this man and this woman in holy matrimony; which is an honourable estate, instituted by God, signifying unto us the mystical union that is betwixt Christ and his Church. . . ."

Wedding vows. Fear cut into her mouth, her muscle. In these vows, marriage was forever – terminal. Terminal illness. The voice pulled her towards itself, pulled her to the window, pressed her against the glass. Face, palms, breasts. The heat was oppressive; her thin cotton t-shirt wedged itself in sweaty ridges under her armpits.

He began reading the woman's vows, a softening in his voice. The words whispered, fragile. Whispered: love, honour, obey. Sweat beaded her face. She tasted salt as she opened her mouth. To protest. Opened her mouth into the shape of "O." Obey. Obey.

Moisture under her palms. The glass warm, seems to mould against her palms. Hands soften the glass, move through it. Into the night air, the night. Into him.

She screamed, pulled back, ran for the phone. Outside, the night stretched, strained against itself, snapped tight like an elastic as the police arrived, searched the area with flashlights. He was gone.

The next three nights, the police hid out, watching her yard. She knew they were there because he was not, though she listened for the voice between midnight and five a.m. The fourth night, the police must have given up.

He reread the text, gentle through the woman's vows, strident through the man's, triumphant at the finale. "Let no man put asunder. I pronounce them man and wife."

Liz did not watch as he smoked his last cigarette. Seven a.m. found her huddled under her bedroom window, curled inward, salt tears burning the skin on her knees.

She opened the mailbox, squinting at early morning clouds. Promise of rain. What are they – thermonuclear clouds? No, that's mushroom clouds. Thunderheads of some sort? What are the names for that cloud formation? Rain The Asshole Away clouds?

Humour sat like indigestible bread pudding around her heart. It was cold out. So were the insides of the mailbox.

It cut straight into her palm. The pain. Blood running down her hand, her wrist, into her housecoat sleeve. Don't stare at it dummy. Get a towel around it. You fucking idiot. Move.

Bound tightly within a tea towel, the throbbing lessened. Liz reopened the mailbox cautiously. A large bread knife sat between the pages of a small black leather bound book, the blade directed upward. She pulled them out gingerly, avoiding her blood on the blade. It was a book of legal ceremonies, more blood smeared across the section of wedding vows.

There was something else in one corner, a burgandy velvet box. She opened this third object in the kitchen, found inside, set with three diamonds, a wedding ring.

That night, as she pulled open the curtains, she noticed the withered edges of M and Ms, felt annoyance stir somewhere in her. Why did these plants struggle so long for green, resist the inevitable brown streaks?

On the counter, the knife lay, its edge a cool glimmer, black lines of her blood decorating its surface. Four stitches lined her palm. She had had to type with one hand at work. They had not been impressed, told her to take a course on cutting bread.

The phone rang, its brilliant sound startling. She picked it up too quickly, jabbed the cold speaker against her ear.

"Hello, Sarah." Try to register. It's Jim . . . on the phone, phoning you. "Or should I say, Liz?"

"Sarah would be fine." Steady the voice.

"I followed you home and then to work. Someone there . . .. Marlyss . . . told me your name. Thanks . . . Liz."

"I'm sorry. I'm just a very private person. I do care for you, Jim. Really."

"Mind if I call you Liz from now on?"

"Sure. Whichever you like. The last name's Sturgeon."

"Erickson, more like it."

"Okay, Erickson."

She took her phone in the next day, had it disconnected. Then bought a darker pair of sunglasses. June seemed to have turned her eyes on fire.

Marlyss stared at the Chev's two flat tires. "How long've they been flat?"

"I dunno, a coupla weeks."

"I'm surprised you haven't fixed them."

"Look, if you don't want to take me, I can take the bus." The sun is so bright. Look down.

"No, Liz – that's not what I meant. You should know that." Marlyss sounded upset.

"Yeah, sorry. I've got a headache." They climbed into Marlyss's Toyota and drove to the mall. The furniture store was close to the south entrance.

Marlyss pointed to a vivid red sofa. "That'll change the mood at your place," she said brightly, more brightly than the sofa, which squawled.

Liz moved over and touched it. "Too smooth," she said. "It doesn't matter what it looks like. It needs to feel . . . oh, I dunno."

"It doesn't matter how it looks?" Liz did not answer. In this thick light, things became too difficult to explain. She moved through the display of living room furniture, touching different objects with her fingers. One sofa gave way, warm, springing back lightly, its surface like velvet. Liz sat down in it, smoothing her palms, then her face, against it.

"It's kind of expensive, Liz," Marlyss said dubiously. "And it's emerald green. Your living room's done in blues."

"I'll take it."

The gallery on Whyte Avenue had too many windows. Liz peered through the sunglasses.

"I want to touch these," she said to the attendant.

"I don't think that's allowed," he said, doubtfully. "It's my first day here – I'll go ask the supervisor."

"Liz, you don't do that sort of thing in art galleries. What's the matter with you?"

"I'm buying – not you."

"I'll be back in a minute." The attendant slid out of the room.

Eyes closed, Liz gently touched an oil painting. Her fingertips traced a sky that pulsed with clouds, grass that scrabbled to get away from wind. The small farm house at its centre felt like a blood clot.

Opening her eyes, she located another oil. This one showed a woman on a swing, her skirt blown up over half of her face. Liz followed the woman's form over the wind-swung skirt, ruffled in smooth waves, then down the body. She ran her fingers over the body area again, eyes still closed. Though the woman wore no underclothes, Liz could not tell where the dress ended and the crotch began. For that matter, the body blended into the sky. No crotch – effectively, the woman had no crotch, at least as a textural difference. This is a place to go and be. She traced it again. Through your fingers.

"Liz, open your eyes," Marlyss hissed. "D'you have any idea where you're touching her?"

But the leaves from the tree stand out. So does the dress and the swing.

Abruptly, Liz dropped her hand. She chose two sculptures. One curved, rounded and porous under her palm, the other smoothed to jagged edges – the feel of water, frozen to ice points. And the second oil – the safe one.

Marlyss helped her carry them into the house, set the painting down on the kitchen table. "Liz, you embarrassed me," she said. "I'm going home now. I did not enjoy this trip with you. I think you're getting weird, or something. And it's kind of dark in here." She stopped, sniffed the air. "What's that smell?"

"What smell?" Liz asked diffidently, tracing the jagged edges of the smoother sculpture. The sniffs progressed into the living room, terminated in a shriek. With a sigh, Liz set down the sculpture and went into the other room.

Marlyss was holding a dead plant in her hands. One of the drapes had been yanked open so quickly, it still swung gently. Marlyss was poking at the plant.

"You like The Sahara?" Liz asked, running her fingers up and down the door frame. The wallpaper curls back into rough edges against the panelling. Funny I haven't noticed that.

"Liz – did you do this to these plants?" The voice trembled.

"Do what?"

Marlyss set the plant down. The saucer clattered on the sill as its rough landing balanced itself out.

"You'll chip the paint, Marlyss. I like that sill – it's the smoothest one in the house, y'know."

Light as cobwebs, Marlyss brushes past, then turns in the open doorway. She is pastel, transparent; the trees behind her imprint on her dress and body like a designer's pattern.

"You need help, Liz. You really do. I don't know what, but this isn't normal . . . natural.

"I just need some sleep," Liz said, wanting to brush Marlyss away, like hair that teased her eyes. She listened to her friend run down the three steps, along the concrete walk. Her heels made sharp clicks – not the round softer circles of sound his footfalls had made the first night. As she pictured

Marlyss making a quick navigation to her car in the hot pink high heeled shoes, Liz giggled. You have to give them credit – those women who live so high on their feet. Takes a lot of athletic ability, effort, and concentration. Probably they take anabolic steroids.

Closing the door, she shifted the sunglasses closer to her eyes. Even with the curtains drawn, it was light in here. She would have to buy thicker drapes. The sofa would be delivered on Wednesday. Time for sleep, but first, feed the plants.

She could do it with her eyes closed. It was simply a matter of pouring the Mr. Clean around each withered stalk. They don't miss daylight anymore. Each day, Chocolate Bunny's stem pushes more sharply against my skin. She smiled, sniffed gently for the smell of lemon.

"He had backed her against the wall and was fisting her, ramming his black gloved hand into her soft cave. Her screams excited him as did the blood that covered the glove. He let her go so that she collapsed to the floor and tried to crawl from him. He stepped on her hair and kicked her and she rolled over, lying helplessly on the floor, staring up at him. In his hand he held a large knife.

"She was too weak to move. Moaning, she felt him kneel above her, saw the knife's edge come closer. Gently, he traced its blade along her chin, down her throat. It began to dog lightly along her collar bone, created a delicate network of pain over her breasts. Thin bright lines of sensation intermingled oddly with the black gloved hand that masturbated her gently. Her head moved from side to side. The sensations confused her. Pain and pleasure danced their slow lovers' waltz.

"As the pleasure mounted, the knife dug deeper across her abdomen, her breasts. She did not notice this, feeling only the intensity of her desire for greater sensation, her need for the dark man and what he could give her. The gloved fingers were inside her now, meeting her deeper need for fulfillment. She arched against him, against the blade, driving herself. Finally, as she felt the orgasm catch her in the centre of swirling circles of pleasure she had never realized possible, she sat up against him, driving the knife he held into her heart."

His voice had traced itself across her skin's surface – light lines that drove deeper as the story progressed. She had begun moving the knife's blade across her lips, then followed his voice down her throat to her breasts, abdomen. Masturbated herself. At the story's climax, the knife paused above her left breast. She shuddered, staring at its cool line of steel. Felt the narrow lines of blood tickling the surface of her skin. Shuddered again, placing the knife down. Tense, tight without the release of orgasm. Lying on the bed, she masturbated, twisted as her need increased. Not able to satisfy herself, she lay awake till morning.

"We have brought this matter to your attention several times now, Liz." Larry's voice was gentle. "The matter has risen beyond our ability to overlook any longer. I think it would be wise for you to resign within the next week."

It had been there again in her work – images of oral sex, violent eroticism. When she did meet his eyes – the blue of blueberry yogurt – her own felt as direct as the knife's edge. "It's not professional," she said, "is it Larry, to let one's peripheral vision interfere with daily life?"

"I don't understand."

"D'you have a scrap piece of paper?" He handed her a used envelope. She scribbled some words on it. "Here's my resignation. I don't think there are any sexual overtones in it. Am I free to go now?"

"Marylss would like to talk to you."

"Ah yes, but would I like to talk to Marlyss?"

He frowned. Liz shrugged and walked out.

Marlyss waited beside the coffee machine. Her voice

fidgeted, twitched. If she turned her head slightly, Liz could keep her friend in profile.

"Please believe – I tried to stop this. I don't understand what's happened . . . to you. To us."

Liz's complete lack of interest blurred Marlyss' face around the edges. "You live with terror, Marl," she said, "it owns you. It becomes your own – you taste it, feel the way it curls into you. Closer than a friend."

There was low, confused moan. "Maybe I've been wrong . . . for a long time. Maybe we've never been friends." Marlyss turned, drifted out of Liz's vision. Her own silence suddenly fragile, Liz rubbed her temples, stared at the coffee machine.

"It's in the corner of your eye, Marl. Somewhere along the line, I dunno, I guess I started looking sideways . . . too much. Things shift. Things play games with you."

But Marlyss was not there. Liz took off her sunglasses, trying to find her. In the heavy office lighting, her eyes stung, filled with tears. She was suddenly afraid. She turned, ran awkwardly to the nearest exit.

Hot for July. Jim held her hand, tightened his grip as he asked, "Why did you disconnect your phone?"

She shrugged off his tone. Her own words came out rehearsed, like the prearranged movements of wind up dolls. "I dunno, Jim . . . y'know me. Nothing personal. I care about you, very, very much." He moved away from her kiss. "Aw, c'mon, Jim – if I could explain it to you, I'd explain it to myself."

Silence. He stretches it out. Does he enjoy the tension? Why doesn't he stop it? The hand grips too hard, too close.

"You going to move now, too?"

"No. Of course not. That house is my Fortress, Jim."

"Against what? Why do you need a fortress? What're you fighting?"

"I'm not fighting anything, Jim. No need to get mean about it." His hand hurts.

"Look at me, Liz. No – straight on. Not sideways. I'm here, right in front of you. Look at me – in the eyes."

Break away. Break away from him. Too close – can't breathe like this. His eyes too close.

She was crying, huddled against the park bench. His arms circled her; their silence cradled pain.

"I love you," he said. She kissed him, eyes closing, felt him respond. They rolled in the grass; skin become sensation.

"Make love to me here," she murmured. "I want you here."

"In the park?!"

She was unzipping his pants.

"Someone'll come. Liz! What're you doing?"

"C'mon, let go Jim. Let's do it here. Under the sky. It's getting dark."

"Stop it!"

He pushed her away angrily. Suddenly, she felt her own anger. Explode. Her hands became birds, flying at his body, tearing at his shirt.

"But I want to. Now. Here."

His hands grab your wrists. His eyes angry. Don't look at them. They don't understand. They don't understand anything at all.

I'll drive you home," he said. "Don't worry – I won't ask to come in. I don't understand you, Sarah Liz. I don't understand you at all."

He stops at the bedroom window.

The knife so smooth. Its edge smoothest of all. Not so hard to face the edge in the end. Not its final superb entry, after months of foreplay.

Quietly to the west door. Unlock and leave it, standing wide open. Heat winds around the sweating body. Drop the thin nightie on the floor just inside the bedroom door.

Feel him at the window, the bedroom window, pressed against the glass. Turn on the overhead light, feel him pull back a little. Just a little, a few inches.

Hard to adjust eyes to the light. Try. Try. Pull the curtain aside. He sees. Drop the head back, feel the eyes slide over skin, through to the bone underneath. Knife in the right hand – move it gently over outer thigh. Bring it up, caressing skin surface. Masturbate with the left hand.

Cut across the breasts slowly, gently. Remember to keep it slow, gentle. His breath, in the dark, feel it, strong, quickening.

Suck on the knife. Feel it cut into the tongue, the warm blood pulse inside the mouth. Run the edge against the neck, at the back. The orgasm wraps itself inside, tight. Releases, violent. Look out, straight into the centre of darkness. Bleeding from the mouth. Hold the knife between the breasts, turn off the light. Into the bed, crawl between the sheets. Curl tight, back to the open doorway. Wait.

He is there suddenly, without sound, in the bedroom door. Silence. No movement. Then the two steps in.

Turns on the light. Blinding. Eyes tear, unfocussed. Fight with the light, turning toward him. Focus.

There is the face. Calm. Eyes meet. Hold.

Then gone. Clear precise footsteps across the kitchen floor. The click of the lock turned before the door closes, quiet and firm.

Outside, the rain.

travelling away

madness opens up in the head
a fan,
a spring of sudden, black flowers.
the tapestry of thought
unbuttons itself
and dimension is discovered.

skin lost . . .
to walk beyond sanity.
continents slide and divide.
day curls, fetal, into night.
i hover, an astronaut,
just beyond meaning's suburbs,
connected by this umbilical cord of guilt
to reason.
i see purpose
back there between the stop sign
and the convenience store;
its shadow has detached,
floats by me.
it determines its own shape,
unobscured by sun.

here, there is no need
to mesh the two conversations –
word and intent, dialects
of the diplomat.
the chasm between the lines, birthplace,

becomes a fingerprint,
i left behind there,
black hole shrunk down
to a pin's head
and gone.

after she left her husband

she scatters herself across november,
footsteps, petals of a would be peony
that believed in love last june.
in pockets, the wind carries her lifetime,
tosses her, bird seed,
left of her conscious self.
in the bureaucracy of dreams,
the crows leave the corn field.
they sense a heaviness to the wind.
it comes, bearing gifts.

mirror images run together.
like wet paint, eyes dribble into mouth;
she thought the face would last.
what does she do with dying flowers
he delivers every day,
the scent of fresh cut
so out of season?

there are moments when
the hand that holds the coffee mug
is hers,
she can feel her own skin.

"victim" takes a passive verb

"the victim was assaulted . . ."
(by fate, i suppose
and by our assumptions)

"the victim grew up,
an average child . . ."
(did she know this would be
her fate?)
"displayed no abnormal tendencies . . ."
(but of course, on some level,
she knew . . .)
"enjoyed ice skating, girl guides . . ."
(putting in time)
"was nominated for . . ."
(boy, was she ever)
"was known for her outgoing,
positive outlook . . ."
(even though she knew she was moving,
was being drawn toward
the car in the parking lot)
"and had recently begun work
as a CBC radio broadcaster . . ."
(unusual – kind of feminist
for a rape victim.
denial interplay –
the last, weak struggles
to escape . . . saw fate coming)

"after the victim left her apartment . . ."
(here victim gets an active verb,
moves like a fish, hooked,

toward fate)
"she went to her car
where the serial killer waited . . ."
(irresponsible, really –
she could've taken the bus,
called a friend.
there was no real reason
why she had to use her car
that day,
why she chose to use her car
that day)

"the victim's car was found . . ."
(it always was the "victim's" car.
that's why she bought it)

"the victim's bedroom window
overlooks the parking lot . . ."
(giving her an appropriate perspective
on her future –
she must've memorized every inch
of the set up,
knew her lines)

"this tragic end . . ."
(she knew she deserved it)

(we know we deserve it)

(victim takes an active verb)

looking for the second face

it's like walking down whyte avenue
with your eyes crossed;
everyone with two faces –
one slightly behind the other
and below.
you know this is the place
for the yuppies and the university kids,
and you're looking for the runaway
kid from the youth center,
under age prostitute.

she's about shoulder height
to the leather jacket swagger
and the social worker frown.
her brain would fit into your mouth.
you could wear her face
as an amulet
or necktie.

it's her face
behind and below –
the one that fades
as your eyes focus
on the surface of bricks,
glass eyes.
it's her face
you're looking for
in the comic and video game joints,
behind the hotel windows
between the repertoire theatre
and health shops.

she is shadow;
the girl opposes man,
must go down as he rises.
everything about the street kid
is metaphor to the middle class –
pain in the ass,
broken shop windows,
the youth emergency shelter.

i've never heard a woman
use rape as metaphor.
i've never seen a street kid
pull hope from her pocket
and spend it on
her future.

story hour

the raped girl reenacts.
she takes the face in the mirror,
smashes it to more realistic proportions.
now each silver thin penis
reflects a minute of her life,
her face . . .
that minute, that hour,
that took on the clock,
years,
that erased the line between
it's over   and
time has unbuttoned itself.

the glass penis
is an artist.
it sketches the bright red vagina
that runs, wrist to elbow.
the raped girl is a body
of hidden vaginas;
the glass penis will hunt
them down.
on the forearm's canvas,
she is again penetrated,
as she was penetrated.

this is the truer rape.
nobody can say it is not
a wound, or
that she is not responsible.

YEA THOUGH I WALK

Gwen twisted in the soft bed, trying to ignore the sliver of street light that underlined the hem of the curtains. She had to be up at 6:15 with the group home's first riser, who had an abysmally early school bus to catch. Groaning, Gwen swung her feet to the floor and sat, chin in hand, staring moodily down. Tomorrow meant a meeting with a social worker, and a dental appointment for one of the girls. A new admission, due to arrive at 4:00 p.m. would entail the listing of clothing, possessions, the assessing of attitudes, potential. All of this required a minimum of shut-eye. Gwen did not usually have a problem sleeping during live-in shifts. With a sigh, she pulled on her housecoat and wandered down the hall to the kitchen.

Her feet paused at Karen's door. The girl had returned that evening from a few days at the locked unit. Last weekend, she had slashed one of her forearms twice. As soon as a bed space opened up, the agency would move her to a locked unit for a lengthy treatment period.

Gwen tried the door handle. It was locked. She frowned, fished around for the house keys in her pocket and unlocked the door, her muscles tensed against the click. In the dark, it always sounded louder. She turned the knob and eased the door open.

At the ravine's edge, the girl stands, looking down. The weight of her name lifts off her like a great, white bird. Its absence carries relief. In the sun, the narrow sides of the dried up river bed are a series of greens, shifting in the breeze. She hesitates, then begins the climb down.

Midway, she stops to rest, sits with her back leaned against a fallen tree trunk. The wood has cracked, its inner baldness showing under the curling bark. Thoughtfully, she traces the circling of a wood knot; it nibbles against her fingertip. The sun's heat, pressed against her blue cotton dress, takes the definition out of her joints, so that she feels fluid.

When she licks her lips, she tastes salt, and runs her tongue further outside her mouth, absent-mindedly. Squinting down the slope, she considers the effort it will take to reach bottom. A breeze blows a strand of her blond brown hair into her mouth and she flexes it against her tongue. It holds no taste.

She continues down.

The curtains had been pushed open and the bedroom hunched in half-light. On the wall, posters of half naked rock stars in tights and teased hair lurked, reduced to black and white by darkness. Karen's giant sized smurfs hung stupidly by their necks on either side of the window, two lumpy shadows. The usual tight constriction circled her own neck, and Gwen swallowed.

The street light fell across the girl's torso, leaving her head in shadow. She had removed the bandages from her arm. It lay, palm up, exposing a long, vertical slash. Gwen stooped to examine it, shoving the predictable fist of panic in her throat aside. Emotions were a frivolity in this profession.

When she had checked Karen at 11 p.m., the girl had been asleep and the bandages in place. Now, Gwen could see the girl had ripped out the stitches. She moved her hand to the shadow where Karen's face lay hidden. They would have to get to a hospital to have someone take care of that arm.

Close to the ravine's base, the girl has to climb through a sagging diamond wire fence. She holds it down as she steps over, but as she releases it, an edge catches on her forearm and tears the skin open. A sudden, vertical flash of pain shoots up her arm. She probes the wrist to elbow cut, the soft red flesh. The blood swells out over the uncut skin; she can see her heart's rhythm. She presses the forearm against the waist of her dress.

On either side, the ravine rises, leaves of trees ducking and swaying. A breeze tosses itself widely across the full width of one slope. The loss of blood makes her sleepy. Dropping her head back, she holds her good arm out and swings slowly around. She hums, low in her throat, enjoys the buzz in lips and throat.

Then her circle staggers and the ground falls up against her. Dark surges around, around, around. Rolls over and runs away. Pushes her head away from her feet. She rolls on the grass, eyes closed, feeling the cool softness cling to arms and legs, the damp smell of ground seep into her nose.

When the dark in her head stops moving, the girl opens her eyes. The trees on the right slope swing a half circle and stop. Flat on her back, she lies with one arm pressed against her stomach, the other flung out. The sky is changing.

A great black cloud rises up over one end of the horizon. The sun is caught somewhere behind it. Around the girl, colours flee. Everything becomes shades of grey. The cloud begins to push itself down into the ravine.

Gwen felt something smooth, slippery, that sucked and pulled at her fingers. It made dry, crinkling noises as she touched Karen's chin and nose beneath it. Quickly, she shifted the thick curtain so that light fell on the girl's head, saw a plastic bag pulled over the head and tucked tightly into the buttoned neck of a flannel nightie.

An immense weariness pressed heavy hands down on Gwen's shoulders, holding her arms against her sides. Slowed the beating of her heart to a single drum beat. It sounded distant insignificant. The silence stretched itself out, curled around her body like a cat, caressing. Breath waited in her lungs. Elastic, the pause stretched further.

Gwen's heart beat again, one quiet thud, and the room was full of young girls, moaning and swaying. Bleeding from jagged slash marks on their wrists. Bruised around their necks. Solvents seeping out of their mouths. They sang, weaving about Gwen and the girl, placing their hands in blessing upon the plastic over the white face, reaching out to touch Gwen's cheeks. Smiling, not weeping. Another heart beat, and they dissolved.

Bending over the girl, Gwen saw how Karen had tied a shoelace around the top of the throat, after tucking the bag into the nightgown. Underneath, the face was pale and slack. Eyes were closed and mouth open. The girl's chest rose and fell so slightly, Gwen could only tell it was moving when she placed her hand on the cold row of buttons between the small breasts.

Droplets of water had condensed onto the inner surface of the plastic; the girl's wiry blond brown hair lay damp around her face. A strand had fallen across one cheek, its ends in the open mouth.

A cry pushes up the girl's throat, wings out into the all around black. Feeling her eyes shift, she touches fingers to her lids to find out if they are open. There is no light now, down here, in the ravine.

She rolls over, pressing her face against the earth. The sense of skin is fading; small blades of grass seem to spread out and blend into one surface. In her nose, there is the faint smell of dirt, warm and moist. She thinks she can still taste salt on her lips. The only sound is the slight pressure a heart beat makes in her ears.

Hesitantly, Gwen extended a hand towards the shoelace that held the bag in place. As she fingered the frayed tips, they felt moist, spongy. Karen had used them to dig into the deep cut once she had ripped out the stitches.

Gwen lifted the other arm, which lay across Karen's stomach. It showed as bloody as the first. There had been no mark on that forearm at 11 p.m. Eyes burning, then blurring, Gwen traced the exterior of the long, wet wound. Her finger, held up to the street light, showed dark on its tip.

They had been so careful to remove sharp objects from her room – agency policy after a girl slashed. Mirrors, tweezers ... they had even taken pens and pencils. Gwen had never thought of the small plastic casing of a shoelace as a weapon.

She was fighting to keep a professional grip on her hands. Hunched on the bed, Karen must have been at this for hours. In the dim light from the street lamps, she would have watched as the shoelace tip, run back and forth, wrist to elbow, moved further and further down into flesh. Back and forth, back and forth.

Scars from friction slashing like this could rise up, an ugly purple, half an inch off the skin surface for the first few years of healing.

Is she on her back or front? In this dark, it does not seem to matter. But she wants her hand. She wants to touch her hand to her mouth and she cannot get at it. There is something, come from a great distance, and it is holding back her hand.

In this place of nothing, something had taken her hand, has taken her hand away from her.

Gwen replaced the girl's arm across her stomach. Under the hot salt fluid of tears, her face burned. Careful not to touch the bed with the tip of her one finger she tipped her hand to keep the blood that had run down one side of her wrist from staining her sleeve.

Years of this. There had been years of these girls, and there was no end coming. A heart beat, and the moaning, swaying girls surrounded her again. Why were they smiling? The last part that faded was each smile.

Gwen pressed the bloody finger across the surface of her own face so that the fluids ran together. Over her lips so that the two salt fluids ran into her mouth and made her swallow. Hard.

She pulled a chair over to the bed and sat down. She took Karen's outstretched hand into her own, pressing the light warmth firmly. Mechanically, tears ran down her face. A cold breeze from the open window traced the back of her neck and she shivered.

It is so quiet. The silence has solidified in her ears. She

lies on her back again, or thinks she does. Pushing down with her palms, she feels the ground retreat from her skin, become a distant surface. Her legs will not move. They are cold lumps of wax, melted onto the ground.

The ground has moved away and she lies on a blanket of dark. Thick – the air is hard to breathe. It lies in her nose and mouth, refusing to move, coagulating. Heavier and heavier, the air, the stuff in her nose, filling up her mouth.

She wanted to move her hand to her mouth, to find out what is in it, but something held it back. Now, she cannot feel her hands. No mouth. They are gone, merged with the all around black. A cocoon of black.

Gwen laid the limp hand on the bed. She had been rocking herself gently on the chair – carefully, so that she would leave no signs of her presence. It was still night outside – no grim reminders of dawn on the horizon.

Gwen sat a while longer, looking out the window. In the morning, there would be an outcry, but they could pin nothing on her. This was not a locked treatment setting – she was supposed to sleep all night. A day on this job demanded a good night's rest.

Gwen returned the chair to its place beside the desk. She walked stiffly to the door, turned and glanced back at the still form on the bed. The head lay in darkness, one arm crossed over the stomach, the other lying palm up, forearm exposed, just as Gwen had found her.

Just as Gwen would find her. Briefly, she wondered about fingerprints on the door handle, but she realized she could say she had left them there when she came in to wake Karen up at 7 a.m. Three hours away.

Gwen locked the door from the inside, and quietly closed herself out.

face without a verb:
meditation of the montreal massacre

it's the face that haunts me now –
its disappearance from the human race.
in the mirror, the eyes, the nose,
the mouth are still there,
and on the magazine covers . . .
but on the street,
in the supermarket,
expressions are all leaving
nouns on the bone.

the radio voice rips the air,
my paper thin face
off in halves each eye
singular hemispheres.

the mouth contains
the initial disbelief –
a black verb, it swells
to accept the moving in
of silence.
there are no nouns.
this has nothing to do
with communication.
the words have crawled away,
ashamed of their meaning.

did they hear the gun shots?
did they hear the shadows
of the gun sound stretching
back to their youngest ears?

did they jump, more than average
at the backfiring car,
the city siren's bloody wail?
over the cafe table,
we are mid window shadows
under sun.
"this man killed fourteen women,"
i say. he winces,
a gentle man, elucidates:
"i wish you would say 'people',"
he says, and he is wise
in his abstractions.

but this 'person' was specific:
"you're all feminists!" he cried.
the gun's face, the gun's mouth –
it defines subject
to object,
singular hemispheres.

even after death
the language possesses.
'his victims.'
did they hear the shadows of definitions
whispering in younger ears?
'man'//'woman':
nouns without a verb.
grammar does not allow
for change within the noun,
though the possessive moves
in on victims.
'his.'

in the church window,
we give him the black metal outline,
divide it into fourteen smaller shapes,
each its own brilliant colour
of blood stained glass;
on sunny days,
we worship there.
'his.'

the face forced into the form
of fashion magazine photograph
newspaper victim photo,
has an identity within its fist
and it remains, static,
a surface definition.
underneath expressions
are leaving nouns
on the bone.

skull is noun.
face moves over bone,
expressing verb.
body becomes corpse becomes deadwoman,
though he can't kill the noun
that never lived in the mind
of the gun's person.

definitions have one exit.
not constructed for much movement,
they define departures of more
than one to a line.
walls, arguments, philosophies
need several escape routes.
university classrooms require
walls of doors,

trap doors beneath every desk,
a secret button
in each student's hand.
this presents advantages, i suppose
in emergencies of fire, too.

every media day,
another 'incident' of assault,
defined as event,
isolated to noun,
but 'past,' 'present,' and 'future'
are in a kaleidoscope,
and 'now' is verb.
sexual assault cannot be noun,
a product like 'chair,' 'toy,' 'pen.'
if it is noun, separate,
isolated to incident,
why do i fear all night streets,
every unlit room
in memory
or possibility?

let's try the headlines
the gentle man's way:
'person' sexually assaults
and murders 'person'
in the subway.
or 3 'people' gang rape
one 'person.' no.
a crowd hoots and shouts –
a crowd of 'people'
watch 'person' rape 'person.'
and the homicide/suicide:
'person' shoots 'person'
then shoots self.

this vocabulary must make us
feel better – words
can be such a relief;
both offenders and victims
become 'people.'

breasts, vagina are gender specific,
the shapes before
the kaleidoscope begins purpose
where hemispheres converge
there are no nouns on bone.

nouns are verbs;
we move within our skins,
and if there are only seven
layers to skin,
why do most wounds
not define in scars?
there are marks at throat,
wrist, mind,
the living skin does not
trap to form, to noun,
leaves twisting under skin.
but the bullets –
they leave their design
in dead motion.

i phone a friend
who has not heard.
it's like passing the buck;
if i can trap the realization
into nouns,
the verb in my head
will become word size.

we measure time
by the days it takes
to forget.
we call this 'healing'
not 'forgetting.'
but the scars of the eighth skin –
they are verbs,
will not be defined
to the past tense.

but let's try it again,
to be fair.
"you're all persons!" he cries
and shoots their faces off.

sorrow has small hands and feet
but anger has claws.
when it gets out

it will be verb.

Beth Goobie

Beth Goobie was born in Guelph, Ontario in 1959. After working for a year in Holland as a nanny, she moved to Manitoba to pursue concurrent degrees in English Literature at the University of Winnipeg and Religious Studies at the Mennonite Brethren Bible College. She graduated in 1983 and spent the next six years working with physically and sexually abused children and teenagers. It was during this time that she began to tap her creativity as a writer, enrolling in creative writing courses at the University of Alberta. In 1987 she won first prize in the *Edmonton Journal* Literary Competition for long poem, second place in 1988 for short poem and first place in 1990 for short fiction. She was also one of the winners of the CBC's "Write-for-Radio" competition in 1991.

In addition to this, her first book to be published, her work has appeared in several Canadian periodicals. She has two other books geared for young readers that will be released in late 1991 and early 1992: *Jason's Why* and *Group Homes from Outer Space*.

Beth currently lives in Edmonton.

Printed in Canada